The Pekinese
Who Saved Civilization

By Sir Addison Silber Howell, Esq.
(AS TOLD TO TRISHA ADELENA HOWELL)

Most photos by Trisha Adelena Howell
Edited by Derek Evan Howell
Financed by Dean Edward Howell

Howell Canyon Press
P.O. Box 448, Tonasket, WA 98855
2003

Blessings!

ADDISON

and

Trisha Howell

Available from Howell Canyon Press:

Books by Sir Addison Silber Howell, Esq.
Isn't this great one enough?

Books by Trisha Adelena Howell
Fiction
You're Mine
Deed of Love
The Courtesan
Magical Heart

Poetry
Living in a Glowing World

Children's
The Princess and the Pekinese
The Adventures of Melon and Turnip
The Poopy Pekinese
The Fart King

Books by Dean Edward Howell
Nonfiction
NeuroCranial Restructuring: Unleash Your Structural Power

The Pekinese Who Saved Civilization is Addison's first book. He invites you to reprint small excerpts but asks you please not to copy the whole book or to sell any part of it without his written permission. He is counting on profits from the sale of this book to buy him endless filet mignons as well as to start a charitable effort to benefit dogs in his area and hopefully (if he can sell enough books) nationwide.

Text channeling and most photos by Trisha Adelena Howell

Additional photos by Michelle Miller **info@admiringanimals.com,** (888) 828-4959

Digital imaging by Richard L. Wells

Edited by Derek Evan Howell

Financed by Dean Edward Howell

Copyright ©2003 by Trisha Adelena Howell

Book Designer: Peri Poloni, Knockout Design, www.knockoutbooks.com

Published in the United States by
Howell Canyon Press
P.O. Box 448
Tonasket, Washington 98855
(888) 252-0411
http://www.howellcanyonpress.com
info@howellcanyonpress.com

Publishers Cataloging-in-Publication Data

The Pekinese Who Saved Civilization/ written by Sir Addison Silber Howell, Esq.
    (as told to Trisha Adelena Howell) p. cm.
Summary: The greatest dog who's ever lived solves all personal and planetary problems.
        ISBN 1-931210-07-1
[1. Dog—Fact. 2. Canine Philosophy. 3. Addison the Amazing]

Howell, Addison Silber (1986-)
Howell, Trisha Adelena (1962-)
Howell, Derek Evan (1983-)
Howell, Dean Edward (1954-)

Published in the United States of America
Printed by KNI, Inc., Anaheim, California
First edition August 2003

We are members of Publishers in Partnership—replanting our nation's forests.

Contents

ADDISON SOLVES PERSONAL AND PLANETARY PROBLEMS

Acknowledgments

Thanks to Larry Silber for waiting on me during my early years and to Trisha Howell for doing the same now. They have both been good servants (rare, since it is so hard to find good help these days!). Dean Howell has also done an acceptable job of supporting me in the posh lifestyle that I have always deserved and easily became accustomed to. And he is this book's executive producer—he showed me the money.

Thanks also to Dawn Monet, who for many years prepared my "gourmet" diet (organic raw emu with veggies and beet juice—boring though it was!), and to "Grandma" Frances for lavishing attention and food on me whenever I'm with her.

Much gratitude also to "Momma" Bernie Wells, who feeds me a variety of organic raw meats (Yippee!), brushes my fur (Who cares?), cleans my teeth and ears (Why?), clips my nails (Ouch!) and administers many of my supplements (Yuck! Why do I have to eat that crap?) and bubble baths (Double yuck!). Nevertheless, Bernie is kind and docile and thus is a perfect servant to me. Thanks also to her husband Rich who scratches my ears and gives me a solid shoe to wipe my face on. Rich has labored in the honored task of digitizing my photos—how nice for him that he's gotten to work so much with my radiant face! Blessings are thereby upon him.

"Momma" Susie, "brother" Brandon and Rosie (Australian Shepherd/ Border Collie mix) Howell have also been indispensable, periodically providing me with a loving home full of greasy food and bones from 1998 through 2000 when "Momma" Trisha and "Daddy" Dean had the nerve to travel without me.

Thanks to my friend Doug who pets me, brings me raw liver and takes me outside when Trisha is busy massaging patients and (gasp!) ignores me. And thanks to my friend Hendrika—she opened up the fabulous restaurant Capers in Chelan, Washington just so she'd always have filet mignon tidbits available to feed me by hand.

Thanks to my personal physicians—Dean Howell, N.D., Anita Pepi, D.C., Cody Ames, D.V.M., Gary Le Samiz, D.V.M., Lee Bennett, D.V.M. and Donald G. Gerard, D.V.M.—for attending to me selflessly and thoroughly as they make the maintenance of my health their top priority.

I am grateful to my personal photographer, Michelle Miller, for capturing my radiance on film and to Linda Haglund for doing much of my secretarial work.

Thanks to Lily Biser for finally getting through to Trisha that I needed to write a book and that Trisha should transcribe it for me. I'd been trying for months to tell Trisha this, but she was too busy with her own agenda to listen to me (how self-involved can you be!).

Thanks also to Lily and her husband Sam for providing fabulous gourmet meals during my trips to Los Angeles. I have never been so well fed before—please keep the organic New Zealand lamb, chicken and raw milkshakes coming. This is how I should live all the time!

Finally, thanks to everyone who has ever been nice to me; there are so many of you I can't name you all, but I do remember each of you individually. And thank you, dear reader, for your attention and for the opportunity for me to teach you. You are all helping me save civilization.

DEDICATION

I dedicate this book to all my brother and sister canines who are constantly helping me save civilization.

WORDS OF WISDOM

"Humility is highly overrated."
—Sir Addison Silber Howell, Esq.

EDITOR'S NOTE

"Unfortunately, I was not allowed to do any editing. All my suggestions fell on deaf, furry ears. (Ears that in the past were often infected. Is it any wonder when they are so obstinate and resistant to change?) Sir Addison declared the first draft perfect, just as he had dictated it, and refused any changes. Why I'm being listed as editor of this book is a mystery to me."

—*Derek Howell*

The Pekinese Who Saved Civilization

Introducing Addison

Once upon a time, in a very near land, there was an amazing, fantastic and irreplaceable small dog—Sir Addison—also known as the Assassin, Little Prune Face, the Small Dog and Mommy Boy. He, along with all WONDERFUL DOGS (actually, wonderful and dog mean the same thing), took on the enormous task of educating and taking care of DENSE HUMANS (also redundant) in order to SAVE CIVILIZATION (which was originally established by canines anyway). He got little recognition or thanks (except self-generated) for this staggering task but continued to selflessly devote himself anyway and with great success. He is hereby nominated to the Canine Hall of Fame and is counting on your vote.

INTRODUCTION

I realized early on that my mission in life was to help the human race. Dog knows, they need it. Most of the humans I've met are pleasant enough but not particularly bright. If you don't believe me, take a glance at any newspaper. Humans slander, threaten, beat up or kill each other just for money or power. Puh-lease!

They spend their time rushing from one place to another, barely resting, mostly cooped up in buildings. And look at how they eat—and even try to force us to eat! Salads, dieting, vitamins—yuck! Who cares if most of the food supply is grown in devitalized soil, with chemicals galore and processed until little nutrition is left! Food is fun, and the best way to eat is to gorge until you pass out.

I figure that a whole race who can't even get the basics of food, rest and shelter right is in big trouble and desperately in need of my help.

You ask, what makes me qualified to help? We Pekinese were perfected in the palaces and monasteries of China—refined places of wealth, learning, contemplation and fattening feasts. Remember the great cultural Renaissance that took place a thousand years ago in China? You guessed it—we were responsible. There's a reason why we Pekinese were kept close to the seat of political and cultural power and enshrined with statues outside important places. We advised humans constantly, although they were rarely aware that we were the source of their good ideas.

Which brings me to another problem with humans—most of them have never learned how to communicate. Every intelligent being knows that the best way to communicate is to look at another and to beam your thoughts directly to him/her. All the dogs I've ever met—and even cats too—understand this. It's basic. Yet I've rarely seen a human being who understands. For example, just yesterday I stared at Trisha and did a little dance for nearly an hour before she finally got a clue that I needed to go outside. We're talking *majorly* dense. She's a kind person, usually a good servant and, of course, I love her, but she's definitely not a mental giant.

But I digress from my theme: I am the Pekinese who saved civilization. I don't want you to misunderstand and to think that I mean solely myself. I acknowledge all dogs who came before me, all dogs I've known in my life and any others who may have paved the way for my brilliant success. All Pekinese—and dogs in general—have had a profoundly positive effect on civilization. In fact, it's only our love and wisdom that has kept you humans from destroying yourselves so far. This is common knowledge among canines, and while I will detail some of our brilliant successes, know that the great dogs of the world can and do speak for themselves. It's just that humans are not always listening.

Addison emerges into the light of creation.

Creation

In the beginning, God—the **G**reat **O**mniscient **D**og Spirit—using His/Her own massive vitality, love and intelligence as the generative substance—created the universe and everything in it. Being so filled with bliss and love, the Great Omniscient Dog Spirit wanted to create others who could share in this ecstasy and through whom S/He could reflect on and experience Him/Herself. That's right: the Great Omniscient Dog Spirit is moving through each of us, is us and wants to party. It is just that many beings, like humans, have become so focused on external worries that they have forgotten how to listen inside to the magnificence and wisdom of who they really are—to the small still voice that says "Party on!"

This is where dogs have the advantage. Because we are naturally closer to the Creator, it is easier for us to get in touch with who we truly are and to express this in the world. We embody unconditional fun, love, joy, reverence, patience, acceptance and the ability to differentiate between the odors of thousands of butts. We live fully in the present, enjoying every precious moment of life with curiosity, wonder and endless hunger.

We never murder (we kill only out of hunger or in self-defense), steal (okay, we might take that lone steak), lie (That's not my vomit, honest!) or cheat (but we will take advantage of you at every opportunity—especially if you have food). We do beg—but what choice do we have? We're hungry, and you have all the good food! Yet we rarely hold a grudge and are willing to forgive completely when the slightest amends are made (Give me that steak, and all your sins are forgiven!) We are never materialistic or selfish (except where food and chew toys are concerned).

We focus on what is important in life and let go of the details, always viewing situations from a large and compassionate perspective. We are cheerful, fun loving, grateful, uncomplaining, understanding, tolerant, loyal, warm, companionable and smell great (especially after rolling in dung). We accept and love all kindly beings, appreciating them for who they are (or what they can do for us: Hand over that steak! Scratch my butt!). We judge according to your place in our hierarchy, which is established by brute force: the strongest and cleverest (like me!) rule—not according to irrelevant human standards such as species, race, beauty, color, nationality, religion, politics, gender, sexual orientation, personal habits, wealth, class or fur length. What difference do these things make?

Therefore, it is possible (though unlikely) that a working dog[1] could be as good as a meditative dog and that even a human being could be as good as a dog. After all, we are all one being at the deepest level. Each of us has the capacity for greatness—for rising to any challenging situation with the best that is in us: with courage, love, wisdom, compassion and procrastination. We have the capacity for endless growth, creativity, love for others, pungent bodily odors and wild food fights.

But I'm digressing from the creation story. Here on earth, dogs were placed as the crowning achievement of creation. How do I know this? I can remember it. We dogs have perfect genetic memory that extends both backwards and forwards. That's how dogs were able to see from the beginning that humans would later gain enough power to destroy the whole earth and therefore had to be carefully supervised and guided from the beginning.

We therefore offered ourselves to you humans as pets, guardians and guides. You see this expressed physically through our watching over you and alerting you to any approaching danger we perceive through our superior senses. You feel this emotionally when we are there to comfort you through difficult, trying times.

What you forget is that we are always there as a beneficial mental and spiritual influence, recognizing and inviting you to recognize the best in yourselves as we bring you back to what's important in life while we also beam creative inspiration towards you ("You are getting very sleepy. You will take all the meat out of the freezer and leave it by my bowl.")

History of the World

The history of the world is the mirror of dogs' successes and failures in enlightening humans as to who we are and how we can happily, successfully and harmoniously live together. I readily admit our failures. Dog "euthanasia," dog castration (you try to make it sound better by calling it "neutering" and "spaying"), dog shots (Get that frigging needle away from me!) and dog prisons (you call them "pounds") all result from our failure to educate you properly.

But you humans must admit that you can be really difficult to get through to! So our failures are really your fault. And all successes are to our credit, such as the many great discoveries and inventions that have benefited dogs and humans.

It wasn't Prometheus who gave fire to humanity but Canineus, the great dog sage who realized humans needed it to survive harsh winters. Let me be clear here—fire was for warmth and later for molding tools. It was never intended for cooking, a human perversion. Fresh and raw is the best—notice that this is what we dogs, and all other animals, always choose when in the wild. We never had cancer, heart disease, etc. until we started eating cooked food with you. And, more importantly, our wild food tasted better, See what we've sacrificed to live with you? You should be properly grateful!

Tool making of all kinds was inspired by dogs. You ask: Why then do we dogs not have our own tools? I reply, why have a human and use other tools yourself? *You* are our tools. We benevolently guide and rule over you as the philosopher-kings that we are, using you as servants to achieve ends beneficial for all of us. And we have forestalled any human rebellion by not letting you know that we are really the ones in charge.

Yet we do not rob you of your free will or initiative. Ours is always a gentle, advising influence that you are free to accept or reject. But be warned: it is when you reject our influence that useless arguments (i.e., those not concerning food), famine, environmental destruction, spaying and neutering result. These threaten the civilization we have created and are trying to preserve.

We are behind pottery, glassmaking, metalworking, mining, farming, hunting, shelter building, the waterwheel, windmill, printing press, steam engine, computer and dog biscuits, just to name a few. We invented all ball games, racing, gymnastics, mud wrestling and jumping for Frisbees.

We are responsible for theater (wagging our tails, kissing your hand, looking at you with sad, hungry eyes—it's all a performance), music (which began with barking), dance (which began with chasing prey), painting (patterns left on the floor after eating) and sculpture (poop piles). We lurk behind all developments in higher consciousness, spirituality and laziness.

I could give you the names and life circumstances of all the dogs responsible for these discoveries, arts and inventions, but that would be a whole book in itself. Just remember that your dog (i.e., the dog who owns you), a neighboring dog or even a dog you see on the streets may be beaming wisdom to you and to all of humanity. Stay unprejudiced and receptive as you open yourself to the messages of all scents surrounding you.

Addison the quintessential Pekinese

The Pekinese Race

Before I talk about myself in particular, allow me to tell you something about my race. We were "the greatest canine discovery of the nineteenth century—the Pekingese, one of the oldest and most dramatically altered breeds in the world."[2]

As even the American Kennel Club (AKC) acknowledges, Pekinese hold a place of honor in the dog world. The reason why I say "even the American Kennel Club" is that organization is wrong about many things. For example, it classifies my breed and others' as "toy."

Talk about demeaning! The great thinkers of the world—the Pekinese, Tibetan Spaniel, Papillon, Shih Tzu, Poodle, etc.—are definitely *not* toys, although you may very well be *our* toy. Another irritating thing is the AKC's focus on breeding us to display characteristics that they want. We can handle our own breeding just fine, thank you very much!

One thing they get right is the divisions between classifications. Early on, dogs decided to specialize and thus divided themselves into groups such as sporting dogs, working dogs, herding dogs and thinking dogs. The thinking dogs like myself are, of course, the highest races and superior to all other types of dogs.

If you think this is my prejudice and I am guilty of judging others by criteria I've just said that dogs don't use, let me correct your misinterpretation. Thinking, meditating dogs are naturally superior to others because they design and coordinate the systems under which all others operate and thus are absolutely indispensable. Of course, deep down we are all the same, and none is superior to another. But functionally, thinking dogs in general and Pekinese in particular are the highest manifestation of creation. So you see, I'm not judging; I'm simply stating a fact.

As I was saying, we hold an honored place in the dog world now, and from the beginning we were revered as sacred by the Chinese (what smart people!). Stout little canines with compressed noses were coveted as early as 1000 B.C. while as Pekinese we trace back at least to the Tang Dynasty of the 8th century A.D. Art objects that still survive were made in our honor, and we were worshipped as expressions of the divine (I told you the Chinese were smart!). We were known as Lion Dogs (recognizing our great vitality and courage), Sun Dogs (recognizing our dazzlingly inspiring and guiding influence) and Sleeve Dogs (because the smallest of us would ride in the voluminous sleeves of imperial household members, the better to advise them at every moment).

We both protected and were protected by the royal family. We were so important that the theft of one of us was punishable by death. It was with great regret that we were unable to prevent the British from looting the Imperial Palace in Peking in 1860. When humans enter a violent frame of mind, it's difficult for them to receive our good influence.

However, we know that all things eventually result in something positive, so even the British looting had the fortunate effect of introducing five of us to the world at large. One of us (Lootie) immediately moved in with Queen Victoria and advised her well—look at the tremendous wealth and creativity in Victorian England! I hate to sound immodest by taking credit for our Pekinese brilliance again, but honesty is always the best policy. To further support my case, let me quote an unbiased source.

"Pekingese were not exhibited in England until 1893, when Mrs. Loftus Allen exhibited one at Chester. However, the undeniable beauty and interesting history of the breed placed it in the foreground where it has since remained. The three dogs who were outstanding in the breed's earliest development in the Occident were Ah Cum and Mimosa, termed the 'pillars of the stud book' in England, followed by a large black-and-tan specimen named [Glanbrane] Boxer, so-called because Major Gwynne obtained him during the Boxer uprising in 1900. Curiously enough, Boxer had a docked tail and so was never exhibited. He undoubtedly did more for the breed in the early part of the century than any other Pekingese."[3]

What this doesn't tell you is that Boxer purposely acquired a docked tail because he didn't have time for the frivolities of the show ring. He was too busy working on saving his breed in particular and civilization in general to waste attention and energy on unessential activities. Like all great people (yes, dogs are people too), he focused on what he enjoyed and was good at, pursuing that to the glory of himself and of all beings.

After expanding our numbers in England for forty years, we were introduced to the United States, and by 1909 became part of the American Kennel Club. This is a mixed blessing. Yes, we are given nominal attention in books and at dog shows. And this is not bad. It's the karma of some of us to go out into the public eye and display our incredible physical beauty and regal deportment. This is important. But not as important as working for betterment of humanity in the physical, mental, spiritual and partying realms. That is my job, as I shall soon demonstrate.

But before we focus exclusively on me, allow me to give four more (largely) unbiased quotes that illuminate both my and other exceptional individuals' personality.

"The transplanting of the Pekingese into Western soil has in no way changed his personality. He combines marked dignity with an exasperating stubbornness which serves only to endear him the more to his owners. He is independent and regal in every gesture; it would be a great indignity to attempt to make a lap dog out of him. Calm and good-tempered, the Pekingese employs a condescending cordiality toward the world in general, but in the privacy of his family enjoys nothing better than a good romp. Although never aggressive, he fears not the devil himself and has never been known to turn tail and run. He has plenty of stamina, much more in fact than have a number of large breeds, and he is very easy to care for."[4] What can I say—we're just simply the best.

"Pekingese are dogs of unflagging dignity, independent and arrogant, with an enormous self-esteem. They are adamant in their likes and dislikes, stubborn, yet with the most endearing playfulness for their friends."[5] Bravo!

"According to the rules set by the Chinese Dowager Empress Tzi His, the Pekingese should have short, bowed legs so that it cannot wander far, a ruff of fur around its neck to give it an aura of dignity, and selective taste buds so that it should appear dainty. She omitted to mention other striking qualities, including the stubbornness of a mule, the condescension of the haughty, and the speed of a snail. The Pekingese is a pleasure for those who enjoy the companionship of an amusing, calm, independent dog. Chinese legend says that it is the result of a union between a lion and a monkey, combining the nobleness of the former with the grace of the latter—this is an apt description."[6] No, we're lions and humans are the monkeys.

"Pekingese are the aristocrats of dogdom, with many different characteristics in one little parcel. A fascinating breed, they are lovable, haughty and bold, with a quaintness that is irresistible....Having lovable dispositions, Pekes are not bad tempered as some people have been led to believe....However,...they seem to know they are of royal ancestry and merit due respect from everyone!...They love to romp and play; they can take long walks or sit quietly by your side for many hours, happy just to be near you. They love to go places and are a great source of fun. Alert, seeing everything that is going on around them...Pekingese are rather jealous by nature and like all the attention they can have....Pekes are hardy little dogs with a stamina much greater than their size. The Pekingese is anything but a silk pillow dog, as he is so often pictured. He can romp and play for a long time without tiring easily...It is easy to understand why this tiny oriental dog was the sacred dog of China, and why he is one of the most popular dogs in the world."[7] Pearls of great wisdom!

I was an exceptionally cute baby.

Sir Addison Silber Howell, Esq.

Yes, the AKC is exactly right in the above description; I feel like it was written for me personally! I am dignified and regal in my independence. I always think for myself; no one can lead me around by the nose (except at meal time). I have a healthy self-esteem, am bold, courageous and stubborn. No reason to bend to a servant's will when I know I am always right! I may deign to grace your lap for a short time, but never think of me as a lap dog; I am my own person. I am calm, easy going and cordial. I will check out a stranger who first arrives as s/he may bring interesting information along. But I can't be bothered long with someone who doesn't show any interest in me.

The dog who provided the inspiration for Wendy Boorer's book is also right, though I want to make it clear that my arrogance and enormous self-esteem are fully justified—as is my being adamant in my likes and dislikes—because I am always right about everything. And, of course, I am endearing to those who love me. Trisha goes on and on every day about how amazing I am[8] (must she always belabor the obvious?), and, of course, she's never spoken a truer word.

The quote by the dog who owns Bruce Fogle is also largely correct, though it must have been written by a canine who is jealous of the Pekinese's amazing combination of beauty and prowess, and so s/he said we are slow as a snail while admitting that we are dignified, regal and noble. The latter is correct, but the slow part couldn't be further from the truth. I can keep up with any human, even hiking up a mountain, *if I want to*. And that's the key: I don't hop to anyone's beck and call like some poor misguided canines do.

The Pekinese who own Beverly Pisano are, as is usual for Pekinese, the most accurate in their descriptions. I *am* a born aristocrat, amazingly lovable, bold and alert. And, as I said, I have great stamina. Of course, I'm sacred and popular worldwide. (By the way, this book called *Pekinese* is an indispensable book that everyone should read and have in their library—it's second in importance only to mine!)

I am affectionate but never gushy. I do enjoy a fine romp up the mountain behind our house. I have so much stamina that I can hike 3 miles up and down a mountain, nearly keeping up with the humans I'm with, even though I'm 17 years old. One vet says my heart and lungs are stronger every time he sees me. He also says I'm the oldest Pekinese he's ever seen (that just shows his lack of experience!). Trisha says she hopes I'll live well past 20 before I pass on.

I have news for her: I won't be passing on. I'm doing just fine in my present form, thank you very much, and I see no point in dying, being reborn as a pup and having to go through all my hard work of self-development again. Instead, I'll continue forever, perfect as I am, ageless in my body and my thinking. Although I'm an elder now—and I possess all the wisdom that brings—I still have the energy and vitality of a youth.

You may think that I'm idealistic or even delusional, but I assure you that I'm firmly rooted in the practical. Being born and raised in New York City, I was streetwise from day one. I used to run with a rough gang of dogs, and I'm here to tell you that not every canine is wiser than humans (though most are). Several of my friends were killed darting out in front of cars.

Of course, a city is not conducive to developing one's full faculties and potential, not withstanding humans' great protestations of "culture." True civilization flowers when one has the leisure and peace to contemplate rich life experiences. The frantic, hectic pace of the city barely gave me time to stop and pee on the roses, rather less time to contemplate the meaning of it all and how dogs—and humans—can live to create an excellent life: a life of beauty, truth, goodness and plenty of fire hydrants.

A dog—and a human—needs to be in touch with the earth, to feel the soil under his/her paws and to breathe in the subtle fragrances and energies that emanate from the immediate source of our being, the great and nurturing Mother Dog Earth. Deep in the pristine countryside—among the vibrant evergreens, crisp mountain air and abundant vegetation—is the ideal place to experience nature's subtle energies. That's where I live now—but I'm getting ahead of myself.

When I was a baby, I was cruelly separated from my mother and sent to live in a claustrophobic cage among others who were equally unhappy. It was called a pet store, and I was very lucky that a gal named Bernadette came in one day so that I could adopt her and her husband Larry. Larry was swell, and he and I had 12 happy years together—first in New York City, then in Atlanta, Georgia and finally in Issaquah, Washington.

By the end he'd not only acquired a new wife named Penny, but also a human baby named Isabelle was on the way. Both Larry and Penny are chiropractors, working very long hours, and they inconsiderately left me at home all day, bored and alone. Bored may not be quite accurate as my mind is always active, either observing or contemplating deeply what I've observed. That's right, even when I appear to be asleep, I'm actually meditating on major issues.

But I was frustrated that I had no outside work—no way to be active to benefit others or myself. I became depressed. Finally it became apparent that my life couldn't continue down such an unhappy and unproductive road. As much as I loved Larry and Penny, I knew I had to leave. It took months of beaming thoughts and emotions at them, but finally they got the message and did as I requested.

They put up my picture and an accompanying notice at a grocery store (a truly wonderful place—especially the meat section!), announcing that I was seeking a new living situation. Promptly—just as I had strongly visualized and thus attracted—a lady named Trisha who realized the great value of the canine race saw my photo and immediately knew that I was the one for her. (Actually, I'd already chosen her way before the time she saw—and thought she was the one choosing—me.)

Nevertheless, it was traumatic for me when I left everything and everyone I'd ever known and ventured off with Trisha to my new home. I experienced days of grief and loss, during which time it was impossible for me to eat (egad—that was horrible!) or even to think on my usual philosophical topics.

But little by little, the cheerfulness of my new surroundings and new family comforted and encouraged me to throw myself into life again. It's important to be in the present, to take on every precious moment of life with gusto, determination and delightful dung breath.

Yet this can be difficult in times of great emotional upset—though most humans find it difficult at all times because you are so cut off from your own bodily rhythms and true feelings. It's amazing to me how many of you humans are out of touch with your true needs, desires, goals and genital odors. No wonder so many of you are restless, unhappy or violent. You take on no larger purpose, and you are squandering your talents and potential.

I hope you take this in the helpful, constructive spirit in which it is meant instead of as snobbish criticism. You humans do have a lot of great qualities and, like us, endless capacities. It's just a shame to see you waste them, especially since this makes you uneasy and discontent instead of confident, focused, fulfilled, happy and drinking out of toilets, which is your and everyone else's birthright.

This is what made me sad about Trisha. She can be kind, gentle, loving and generous (generosity toward me is the best human virtue), but she was unfocused and not exercising her talents when I met her. She worked some in Dean's office but seemed to spend most of her day cooking, cleaning, taking care of voluminous mail and fielding phone calls—when all she really needed to be doing was pampering me. She had lots of creative potential but wasn't exercising it. Knowing this in advance, I took pity on her and decided to adopt and help her, even though she repeatedly failed her IQ test with me.

Trisha kept asking me questions like, "Who's good? Who's exceptional? Who's amazing?" No matter how many times I beamed "ME!" toward her, sooner or later she'd ask me again—and she's still asking me five years later! Either she's incredibly stupid or she has a very short memory. Since I love her and want to give her the benefit of the doubt, I assume she has a defective memory and feel sorry for her. Her intelligence and memory seem to have improved some under my tutelage (most of the time she understands my wants much faster than she used to), but I'm afraid she'll never be in my mental league. Poor girl!

Anyway, both Trisha and Dean were living on six pretty acres at the south end of Lake Goodwin (about 40 miles north of Seattle). However, the atmosphere there had deteriorated as more powerboats zoomed across the lake and a housing development came in across the street. The peace and serenity of nature had been destroyed. I knew we had to move to a quieter, calmer place to be able to clearly hear my own inner guiding voice, to gorge in peace and to groom my genitals without interruption.

The problem was, Trisha and Dean were so focused on the busy events in their lives that I couldn't get a thought in edgewise—they wouldn't even listen to their own intuition long enough to realize that they needed to move. I modeled serene contemplation, and Dean pronounced me lazy. I engaged in endless meditation and deep self-contemplation, and Trisha remarked that I sure seemed to sleep a lot. It took nearly nine months of constantly beaming moving thoughts at them before "they" came up with the idea to move and started looking for property in Eastern Washington.

Dean and Trisha found lots of properties for sale on the Internet (What a wonderful machine! Another dog-inspired invention), but I refused to consider anything under 100 acres. It's important to establish a large territory to sniff around and to protect! With my guiding influence, we found our new home on the first day of looking: 200 gorgeous wilderness acres in the middle of 3,000 such acres, complete with meadows, forests, mountains, creeks, horse and cow dung. I was in heaven! Finally, I had a place to exercise, to explore, to develop all my senses!

Besides caring for my property, communing on a regular basis with the spirit of the land and eating cow pies, I inspire Trisha's writing and I assist in greeting and healing patients who come to Dean's office (he's a naturopathic doctor). People get happy just from looking at me and from receiving the positive energy I'm beaming at them. (But I also allow them to pet me sometimes as this makes them feel even better.) Despite all my activities, I still have plenty of time to meditate. I am over 120 years old in dog years, and so I've accumulated an enormous amount of wisdom, which I will share with you in the remainder of this book.

Because of my barkingly good and pantingly amazing accomplishments, I have knighted myself Sir Addison Silber Howell, Esq. to demonstrate my great importance, nobility and wisdom—and therefore the reverence and respect that is my due. However, I recently had the

Addison the Wonder Dog

I am a multifaceted and multitalented canine person. Being over 17 years old (over 120 in dog years), I've had the vast experience and time to develop myself in all directions. You will see a partial list of my accomplishments below.

You too can have accomplishments like mine, if you'll take the time and effort to follow the scent life presents you. Everyone is infinitely magnificent and talented because we are all expressions of the Great Omniscient Dog Spirit. Just listen to your instincts, believe in yourself and leave no scent unsmelled!

Addison the Painter

Here is my latest creation, cleverly painted in what look like ordinary letters. It is deeply symbolic and all encompassing. You can see the whole of life in it if you look at it long enough and from enough different viewpoints.

```
        ADDISON ADDISON
        ADDISON    ADDISON
       ADDISON        ADDISON
      ADDISON          ADDISON
     ADDISON  ADDISON  ADDISON
      ADDISON          ADDISON
     ADDISON            ADDISON
    ADDISON              ADDISON
```

Addison the Sculptor

The perfect material for sculpting is your own poop. First, it is the ultimate tangible expression of yourself. It tells the story of where you've been, what you've eaten and the unique way in which your world within has processed the world without. Second, it is a very malleable medium, very easy to work with. Third, it is created at least once a day and thus is very available. Fourth, it forms a unique work of art every time it is excreted. Here is one of my recent creations—lovely, isn't it? And fragrant too!

Receiving my designation as poet laureate.

Addison the Poet Laureate

ODE TO A COMPOST PILE

Divine fragrant treasure

Abundant beyond measure

The olfactory delight of rotting lamb

The sensory feast of rancid Spam

Melons oozing with slippery slime

Green mold frosting that once was lime

I could forever sing the praises

Of decomposing dumps in all their phases

Like a fine wine enhanced by age

Or a rare cheese in blue moldy stage

A compost pile improves over time

Before it's grime but after it's slime

At the perfect moment it speaks of the past

Future and present, a world so vast.

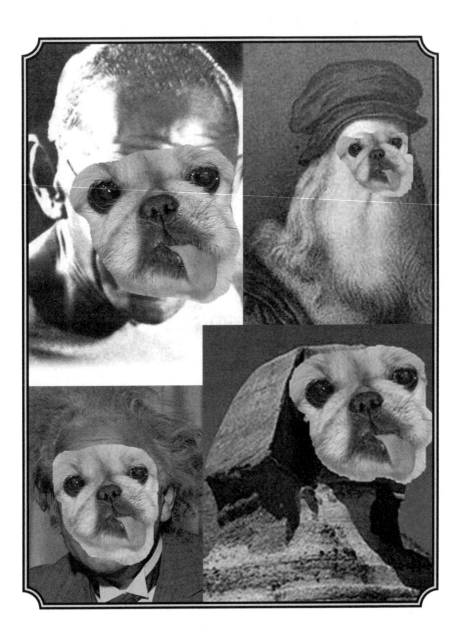

Addison the Impersonator

Yes, I realize my imitative ability is enormous. You must be completely awed at my talent. Here I appear as Mahatma Gandhi, Leonardo Da Vinci, Albert Einstein and the Sphinx—appropriate subjects for me to imitate since I share their genius, wisdom and mystery.

Even though they have no chance of even remotely imitating me, it's only fair that I give my human family an opportunity. Here Trisha and Dean Howell (so-called "Mom and Dad" but more appropriately "my slaves") and my caretakers Rich and Bernie wells try—and fail—to capture the essence of being me, Sir Addison Silber Howell, Esq.

Addison the
Musician and Composer

Here's one of my family's earlier compositions. If it sounds like something you've heard before, it's because a human stole the melody from my ancestors and changed the words. Here I am playing the music while the original words—with the addition now of my name—appear below:

"Home, home in the bowl,
where the food and Addison play.
Where seldom is heard a dieting word
and it's great to just gorge all day."

Addison writes the story of Woh-Woh.

Addison the Storyteller

O nce upon a time, many thousands of years ago, there was a perfect Pekinese (actually, "perfect" and "Pekinese" mean the same thing) born in China named Woh-Woh ("Little Dog"). Woh-Woh was full of love and joy, and he saw goodness, beauty and glorious rotting garbage in everything. But he also saw people bringing strife, violence, selfishness and nail clipping into the world because they had forgotten their connection with the Great Omniscient Dog Spirit and thus their oneness with all dogs. Famine, meanness to one's neighbor and too many baths were threatening the future of the human race. Woh-Woh knew he had to do something to save civilization.

41

Woh-Woh adopted a peaceful monk to help him carry out his mission. They recruited many dogs along the way. Traveling throughout the land, the dogs modeled to others fun, affection, generosity and urinary marking. They saw the best in every person they met and enabled each person to see this beauty within themselves. Soon a movement of loving and joyful feasting spread throughout China and eventually the whole world.

Thousands of years of matriarchal peace and plenty followed—until there gradually arose a patriarchal urge to dominate and control the supply of steaks. By this time, thousands of Woh-Woh's descendents were working to preserve civilization, but humans had become so focused on verbal language that they'd forgotten the original and most powerful form of communication: directly through mental pictures. Humans were no longer conscious of the uplifting pictures the Pekinese and other dogs were sending them, so they could be influenced only subconsciously. This made progress slow and enabled the growling, snarling elements to temporarily take over.

But dogs everywhere kept working, and over the millennia they managed to move society more and more towards a true civilization of fun and feasting. There are now millions of dogs in the 21st century working on this project, and they are confident of their eventual success, perhaps even in this century, if a few humans armed with bombs and hatred don't manage to kill all of us first.

To play or not to play—that is the question.

Addison the Philosopher

Dogness is the essence of all Being, the fundamental substance underlying the fabric of existence that manifests itself through all empirical qualities in the world. Dogness is the most basic, a priori principle from which all conclusions are derived. It's impossible to define dogness since dogness is the ground of all definition. The degree to which a being embodies dogness is the degree to which s/he is explicitly real. All departure from dogness is illusion as the Great Omniscient Dog Spirit is in some form expressed in everyone and everything. We are all One—all expressions of the Great Omniscient Dog Spirit— though some of us are better expressions than others.

Addison the Sage

Do unto other dogs as you'd have them do unto you.

A dog saved is a dog's love earned.

The barking that goes around comes around.

One good bark deserves another.

There's nothing better than the love of a good dog.

Addison the Psychoanalyst

And how did that make you feel?"

Addison the Linguist

I'm fluent in eight languages (English, Spanish, French, German, Italian, ancient Latin, ancient Greek and cat)—here you see me communicating in cat. I'll demonstrate my amazing ability by translating the following sentence:

I'm a very talented dog—I speak eight languages.
Soy un perro muy talentoso—hablo ocho idiomas.
Je suis un chien tres doue—je parle huit langues.
Ich bin ein sehr begabter Hund—ich spreche acht Sprachen.
Sono un cane di molto talento—parlo otto lingue.
Sum canis ingeniosus maximus—loquor octem linguae.
Eimi skulax akribos me talento—lego okto glottas.
Meow meow meow meow meow—meow meow meow meow.

Addison the Athlete

I'm a skilled ball player of all kinds of sports as well as a gymnast, mountain climber and snowshoer. I'm also great at bouncing on the rebounder (mini-trampoline). Just imagine how high I could jump if I wanted to! I would go into the Canine Olympics if I weren't so busy doing more important things like snoozing and saving civilization.

Addison the Model

H ere I am modeling a one-legged version of my famous sphinx pose and here is my sphinx riddle:

What walks on four legs, is unconditionally loving and is the greatest hope for the future of civilization? (Do not answer "cats" or I will be very offended![9])

Addison the Actor

Here I am in the role that Trisha wrote for me as the ditzy hairdresser's dog. If the novel (*You're Mine*) ever gets made into a screenplay and the screenplay into a movie, you will see my extraordinary acting ability. The part calls mainly for me to sit in my bed looking bored. I will deliver the most true to life performance imaginable. In fact, I'll probably steal the movie with my appearance. Dog-ademy Awards—here I come!

Addison the Film Critic

There are two categories of film: movies with dogs and movies without dogs. The latter are without any merit and can be dismissed out of hand. The former have value according to how much screen time dogs occupy and how their moral character is depicted. Films showing dogs bringing happiness, joy or other uplifting qualities into the world generally receive a four-paw (highest) rating.

Films meriting a four paw rating include classics such as "Ace Ventura, Pet Detective," "The Adventures of Milo & Otis," "Air Bud," "All Dogs Go To Heaven," "As Good As It Gets," "The Awful Truth," "Balto," "Beethoven," "Benji," "Big Red," "Bingo," "Call of the Wild," "Dog of Flanders," "The Dog Who Stopped the War," "Fabulous Joe," "The Good, The Bad, and Huckleberry Hound," "Greyfriars Bobby," "Homeward Bound,"

"The Incredible Journey," "It's a Dog's Life," "Kavik the Wolf Dog," "Lad, A Dog," all Lassie films, "Little Heroes," "The Law of the Wild" and all other films starring Rin Tin Tin Jr., "The Lone Defender" and all other films starring Rin Tin Tin, "Man's Best Friend," "My Dog Skip," "My Magic Dog," "Nikki, the Wild Dog of the North," "Oh, Heavenly Dog!," "Old Yeller," "101 Dalmatians," "Poco," "Pound Puppies and the Legend of Big Paw," "Richard and Vivi on Life's Adventure" (a film Trisha wrote and produced about two magnificent canines; unfortunately, it has not been released yet)", "Rover Dangerfield," "The Shaggy Dog," "Sherlock Hound: Tales of Mystery," "Sherlock: Undercover Dog," "Shiloh," "Skeezer," "Son of Rusty," "Sounder," "Summerdog," "Teddy at the Throttle, " "The Thin Man," "To Dance with the White Dog," "Top Dog," "The Trial of King Boots," "Turner and Hooch," "The Ugly Dachshund," "The Underdog," "When Lightening Strikes," "Where the Red Fern Grows," "White Fang," "The Wizard of Oz," "Wolf Dog," "Wolfheart's Revenge," "Won Ton Ton, the Dog Who Saved Hollywood" and "Zeus and Roxanne."

These are just a few of the great dog films. More are listed under "King of Beasts (Dogs)" ('King' is correct, but I don't like the 'Beast' part) in the wonderful *VideoHound's Golden Movie Retriever*, edited by the dogs who own Martin Connors and Jim Craddock (Visible Ink (Gale Research), Farmington Hills, Michigan, 1999). A system of woof! (lowest) to four bones (highest) is used to rate movies. Unfortunately, the actual ratings are sometimes off because they don't operate according to the clear and absolutely correct criterion I detail above.

Addison the Architect

The perfect dwelling is the most functional, while it maintains an ease and pleasure derived from beauty and (what usually amounts to the same thing) proper energetic balance. Feng shui is the human science of correct placement to maximize beneficial energy and well being, but we dogs are able to accomplish the same thing simply by instinct.

Here is a photo of one of the dwellings I've designed. You don't see much of the building because the really important thing is the sign announcing that it's mine and so the credit goes to me. The three important factors for maximizing quality of life are food, a comfortable resting place and a convenient place to poop and pee. There are plenty of steaks and soft pillows inside this building, and there are many places for pooping and peeing outside, so it's another brilliant Addison creation!

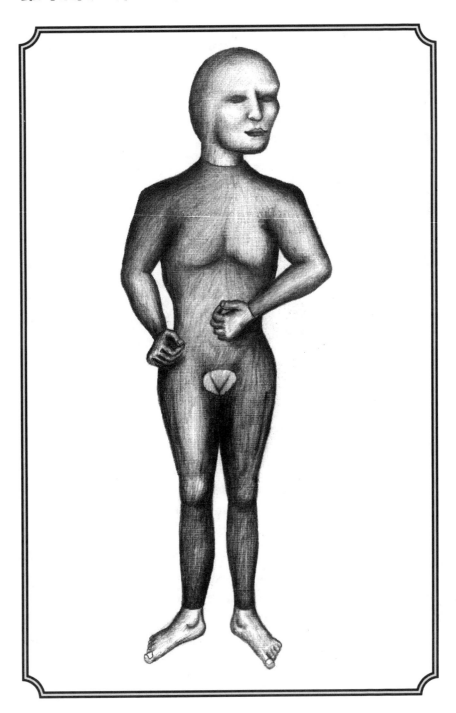

Addison the Fashion Designer

*F*ashion is actually unnecessary as the freest and healthiest way to be is as nature intended. That's why we dogs never wear clothes, unless forced into such indignity by the humans we own. I have only one outfit—my birthday suit—and I look great in it all the time.

For humans, however, clothes are necessary because you have no fur to protect you from extreme heat and cold. Again, functionality is the primary consideration. Therefore, I have designed a highly functional natural garment that is easy to care for and long lasting.

This design is made of heavy-duty organic cotton so that the skin can breathe and yet be kept warm or (in the thinner version) cool. A small amount of spandex is added to maximize comfort and easy range of motion. Note the large hole exposing the genital area, which is highly convenient for peeing and pooping. I've never seen anything like this in human design before, so I can only conclude that humans are not very talented at creating practical clothing.

Addison the Hairstylist

Once again, simplicity and functionality are the best criteria, so here you see the wonderful hairstyling job I did on myself. I decided to go all short to beat the summer heat, and, I must admit, the result is spectacular.

Addison the Gourmet and Food Critic

Food is good, and we should be grateful for all of it, but some food is better than other food. Beef is the best, and steak is the best of the best. But all meat tastes good. It doesn't really matter how or if it's cooked, what cut the meat is, etc. What matters is that it's meat and thus very tasty to carnivores like myself.

Some fresh fruit, like mangoes, is good as are some starches like pasta and brown rice. Vegetables are reportedly very good for you, but who cares; they have no taste! Desserts are awesome: anything with sugar, and especially with chocolate, is worthy of investigation.

Addison meditates on his passion.

Addison the Business Dog

The main thing is to do what you love, and then the food will follow. There is ultimately no sufficient reason to continue doing something you hate, when life is actually about love, joy, peace, freedom, fun and a good steak. Look inside yourself, and ask what your greatest passion is.

When you've determine this—when you find out what makes you feel most alive, creatively powerful and fulfilled—then you'll know where to focus your energies. There is always a way to generate food, shelter, a warm bed and a fire hydrant by doing something you love, if you take a creative enough approach.

After you've found and are utilizing your passion, the other things needed to succeed in business are: focus on the right problem/goal, creative brainstorming for all possible solutions (however outrageous), hard work, clever management of resources (material—efficiently raise and use capital—and human—listen well, ask in a way that you can't be refused, reward often) and cheerful, lavish service to clients.

Take me, for instance. My passion is deep thinking and meditation. The right goal for me is saving civilization. The correct solution at the moment is writing a book to enlighten all who read it so they too can help save civilization. This is also a good way of managing one resource—the reader. Managing Trisha has been difficult, but my constant encouragement and praise of her (albeit meager) efforts has helped. I take easy possession of capital that Dean has raised by working (and to which I'm also entitled because I help treat patients). And I cheerfully offer this book to you, dear reader. See how well my advice works?

Addison the Financial Wizard

One of the fundamental principles of financial management is to avoid excessive debt. Credit card debt is especially nasty; someone else gets rich off the high interest you pay (so no steaks for you!). It's better to lend with sufficient collateral so that you can get rich yourself. Another way to avoid debt is to keep your lifestyle simple. I own a bed, a ball, a starfish and two food dishes—that's it! So my expenditures are very low.

When you have money saved, invest it wisely. High risk, get-rich-quick schemes are a good way to lose all the bones you've made. It's best to make moderate interest (or better yet, free dog food) on safe personal loans, government-backed bonds, t-bone bills and certificates of butcher deposit. Or invest your money in yourself: buy meat and soft pillows then treat yourself and your dog to a steak in bed.

And, finally, remember that it's not important to be rich. The main reason to have money is to buy yourself time to engage in more interpersonal and creative activities like playing with your dog or butt sniffing. Slaving away for long hours is self-defeating. Leisure—not possessions (which end up just weighing you down)—is best. Look at me—I'm so happy, wise and amazing because I've used my leisure to have fun!

Addison the Doctor

You've probably heard people claim that the best medicine is preventive: By living a simple and healthful lifestyle, you can avoid all the misery and expense of sickness. These same people (like Trisha) assert that fresh, locally grown, unprocessed and organic whole foods, plenty of fresh air and daily exercise, frequent pooping and a generally cheerful, uplifting emotional and mental state are the key factors to long-term health and happiness. They say to get into the habit of breathing deeply, stretching every hour and going out into the sun and fresh air every day.

I say baloney. I'll concede that lying around in the sun doing nothing is very pleasant, but the rest of their recommendations are entirely unnecessary and sound like way too much work. My philosophy of life, liberty and the pursuit of happiness is: "Food, fun and f— everything else." Who cares what you eat? Just gorge on any food you find anywhere and don't think about how your lifestyle might be making you or your family sick. What difference does the future make anyway?—just focus on the pleasures of the moment.

The be cheerful part is okay, as long as it doesn't require you to put out any effort or to change in any way. Who cares if playful, joyful and thankful thoughts create positive vibrations that are very good for your well-being? The only thing to consider is that joyful thoughts are fun. And who cares if the quickest way to tear down your health is to poison yourself with any kind of negative thought? Health is irrelevant; fun is not.

Of course, you must recognize problems (see them as opportunities to increase your food supply) and growl about them right away. Don't let anything fester—that's a drag. If you can't change an unpleasant situation, find the unconditional love, joy, peace and canine wisdom that are inside you to be happy anyway—don't let anyone pee on your parade. (Okay, I know what you're thinking, but I AM trying to be happy with the Nazi Twins. I just haven't succeeded yet. Besides, it's so much easier to give others advice than to follow it yourself!)

Trisha keeps harping on this detoxification thing—she says it's important because we've all been dosed with nasty environmental chemicals (auto exhaust, pesticides, excitotoxins[11], construction material out gassing, house cleaning toxins, flea dips, etc.).

So for a week or two a year she does *daily* colonics (not up my butt!), liver & kidney flushes (ugh!), vigorous exercise (actually lots of rebounding[12] is fun—I'm on a rebounder about to jump in the section Addison the Athlete), three hours of low temperature (120-140 degree) saunas (No way—too hot for me!), drinks lots of pure water (poison!) and gets extra rest (finally, a smart idea).

She claims that this, along with a regular healthful daily routine and occasional structural work (like Dean's NCR—see **www.drdeanhowell.com**), will keep you healthy. Also she says not to put anything on your skin that you wouldn't eat—it gets absorbed. (But I'll eat anything!)

Nonsense! And a major drag! I'm glad I don't do any detoxifying; it sounds like a lot of effort! Better to ignore it all and live as unhealthily as possible. Eat, breathe and otherwise absorb as many toxic chemicals as you can. These promote fecal breath and a strong bodily odor, which is delightful. With toxins trapped in your body, your life will be shorter and eventually full of debilitating illness and pain, but don't worry about it. That's in the future. And when you die, just think how well those chemicals will preserve you. Right now just gorge and purge.

We dogs gorge then purge. We eat until we can't stuff another bite down and then, if we don't feel well, we eat grass and let it absorb all the icky stuff. (Humans also do this with wheat grass juice.) Then we either let the grass pass through our digestive system to clean us out or throw it up right away. It is good for us to eat grass; you shouldn't prevent us, even if the grass has been sprayed with toxic chemicals. That just gives us more to purge! Every dog deserves his/her own patch of grass.

Addison the Philanthropist

As soon as I have enough profits from this book, I will establish an organization to benefit domestic animals locally and, if possible, everywhere. Every animal has the right to a pleasant, peaceful life in which ample high quality food, shelter, affection and back scratching are available. Murdering dogs is not a tolerable option. We have benefited humanity in so many ways; the least you can do is provide us with a decent life. We really ask so little in return for our love and wisdom.

Addison with gal pal Lola.

Addison the Proctologist

In case you don't know, a proctologist is a doctor who specializes in the physiology and pathology of the rectum and anus. I'm an expert in this and think that everyone else should be as well. Humans vastly underrate the sense of smell. By smelling anuses, you can determine with great accuracy what your subject has eaten, how her digestive system works, where she's been and the general state of her health. Besides being highly informative, this is also a very fun pastime. I cannot recommend it highly enough!

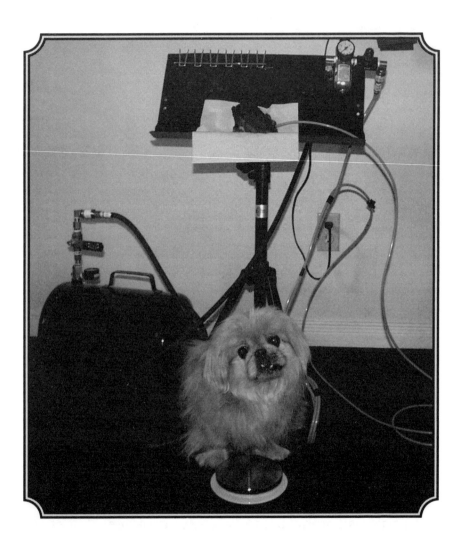

Addison the Inventor

Here is my invention to expand steak. It is very useful! I can double the size of any steak in less than a minute. If I could continue at that rate, within a day I'd have a steak the size of the universe. Wouldn't that be great! Unfortunately, the doubling works only once per steak. But soon I'll work out all the kinks, and there will be steak, steak and more steak for everyone. I'll be hailed as the savior of the world, putting an end to all hunger. Yeah for Addison!

Still, my greatest invention is myself. I've invented myself as an adorable, wise and generally amazing canine being. You too can invent yourself as anything you want. Just focus intently on what you want to be and live each moment as if you were that. If you fake it long enough, with determination and imagination, you'll make it!

Addison the Mathematician

huge (preferably filet mignon) steak+1 Addison=1 happy dog!

Addison the scientist analyzes data while Nazi Twins Alex and Hanna do nothing.

Addison the Scientist

We dogs are great scientists, constantly investigating the world around us with tireless curiosity and enthusiasm. Scientific inquiry is a discipline that requires a good sense of smell. Observation via sight and hearing are necessary, but smell and taste tell you so much more. I've accurately categorized thousands of physical objects by smell and taste alone. Categorization is always directed by and expressive of an agenda: various assumptions and a point of view. I categorize as to how useful—especially, how edible—something is to me. What better aim for science?

Addison locates buried food.

Addison the Detective

A n acute sense of smell comes in handy for a detective as much as for a scientist. Olfactory clues constantly provide you with an accurate and complete picture of anything of importance that's going on.

For instance, I can always deduce when food is forthcoming, when danger is lurking or where it's best to pee by using my amazing sense of smell. And this is all the information anyone would ever need.

Addison the Lawyer

Have you been wronged by someone? Let Addison the wonder dog fight for your rights! When I go into court and argue a case, people take careful notice and really listen to what I say, since I'm the only canine lawyer I've ever heard of.

I'm very reliable and am known far and wide for always being a dog of my word. Also, I can cut through all the legal mumbo jumbo and leap right to the heart of the case, quickly and accurately sniffing out the appropriate law to bolster our cause. Finally, I'm cheaper than most lawyers. I charge only one large filet mignon per hour. So hire Addison to champion your rights! (Hurry up, I'm hungry!)

Addison the Teacher

This whole book is a demonstration of what an amazing teacher I am. Pearls of wisdom drop from my snout on every page.

Addison the Gardener

L ook at the beautiful flowers that grew with my care. I watered and fertilized them daily when sent outside to relieve myself.

Addison the Naturalist

I've amassed a wealth of knowledge about animals, trees, plants, dirt, rocks, rain, etc. through careful observation, especially by smell and taste. You may have noticed that all dogs have this talent and that, for some reason, humans fail to learn about the world around them through the delights of odor and taste.

Another way to learn about the world is to pee on things around you and then smell the result. This works even better if you return later to smell whatever information someone else may have contributed in the meantime.

Addison the Mountain Climber

H ere I am, climbing a mountain as tall as Everest. Note my stamina, my strength, my agility and my chic appearance.

Addison the Snowshoer

Here I am last winter (right), leading the way up a treacherous mountain. I am such a talented snowshoer that I don't even need snowshoes.

However, Trisha insists that I get properly outfitted for this coming winter, so here I am (left) in coat and booties (the indignity of it!).

Addison the World Traveler

Here I am in New York, London, Paris and Rome—all at the same time! I am the only traveler so far who's been able to accomplish this amazing feat.

Ready to answer any question.

Addison the Advice Columnist

Dear Addison,

I'm having a terrible time with the humans I own. They feed me dry, tasteless brown lumps, they leave me alone for most of the day and they barely pay any attention to me when they get home. What should I do?

Sincerely, Spot

Dear Spot,

Scatter such insulting excuse for food all over the house, pee and poop everywhere, chew up all available shoes, shred the carpet and drapes, bark incessantly and bite when ignored. This should get their attention.

Blessings, Addison

You too can benefit from my sagacious advice. Just go to **www.addisonthedog.com** and click on the "Ask Addison" button. I will drop my pearls of wisdom on you for a porterhouse or two.

Addison the Yogi

"**O**m shanti shanti om." Here I am in peace and at one with all life. You too can experience this union with the universe.

They say that yoga is a great way to tune into yourself and to get your mind, body and emotions in top shape. I say it's a great way to rest while pretending that you're actually doing something. (Here I am in my favorite pose: corpse.)

Yoga's also cool because it acknowledges the magnificence of dogs through such postures as "upward facing dog" and "downward facing dog". Give it a try!

Note the halo extending from my whole body in the sheet pattern.

Addison the Guardian Angel

May all love, joy, peace, gratitude, steak dinners and other blessings be with you. May the Great Omniscient Dog Spirit's shining face smile on you and His/Her wet kisses comfort you. May you always be receptive to the wisdom and guidance of the canine kings. May you live in harmony with all of creation.

Addison Solves Personal and Planetary Problems

Here is the heart of my book, for which everything else was just tummy scratching. I will provide you with indispensable advice and guidance for all of life's most important situations.

The Nazi Twins, who I personally think should be discriminated against!

Discrimination Against Dogs and Others

Some humans claim that one of the most urgent problems in the world today is a lack of love or even tolerance for our fellow creatures. They say that differences could be celebrated instead of condemned, and then we would all be a lot happier. They tell us to remember that every creature is a part of ourselves[13], that we share the same basic life energy and that whatever we do to another, we thereby do to ourselves. They believe that when we realize this, we will act with much more acceptance, generosity and respect toward others. And this is supposed to benefit everyone's happiness and character.

Give me a break! Sure, we are all parts of the Great Omniscient Dog Spirit, but you've got to admit that some of us are better parts than others—that's why there's the hierarchy of the pack. (Okay, I said earlier and will again say later that, in principle, we are all of equal value, but maybe I'm just saying this to make you feel good. Besides, why should I be consistent? No one else is.)

I can't see tolerating anything or anyone that irritates me. I know that I'm better than humans, so why beat around the bush about it? Those I don't like must be removed from my glorious presence. Those who disagree, threaten or usurp me in any way must be removed from my country (or maybe even removed from the earth—my planet. Yes, I mean put down!).

Discrimination against humans is no big deal—it's everywhere and still accepted in one form or another by most people (even people who say they are against it). But I am appalled at the discrimination I find against dogs. You humans can be so brutal to us! You don't allow us in most enclosed public places, you use us for experimentation, you eat us, and you even beat up and murder us (for which we have no legal recourse). This is clearly barbaric—a total lack of civilization. See why you need our guiding influence?

Two years ago I was attending Derek's last basketball game of the season—his last high school game ever—and a horrible lady had the nerve to try to throw me out during half time after I drank out of a water fountain. She said, "No animals are allowed in the building." Can you imagine the cruelty and injustice!

Fortunately, Trisha didn't comply with this outrageous demand, but I did have to go back into my Sherpa bag, which means I couldn't watch the rest of the game. And it was a very exciting and close game, as I could hear. What was the nasty lady's problem? I'm cleaner and quieter than most of the other people who attend the game. I'm extremely well behaved and would never consider relieving myself indoors. Some people are totally prejudiced and illogical.

There is so much prejudice to be overcome! And just think of the ingratitude. Here we dogs are, doing everything in our power to take care of you humans and to save civilization. And how do you repay us? By treating us with enormous indignity, by viewing us as chattel instead of the persons that we are. This must change! Dogs of the world unite!

Food arranged to look like Addison.

Food

Food is good; being hungry is bad. I'll eat anything if you'll give me the chance. Who cares that truly nourishing food is fresh, barely processed and preferably locally grown? Who cares that totally organic is best—not only because those pesticides, herbicides, etc. are poisonous but also because commercial produce is grown in devitalized soil where most of the minerals have been depleted and not added back (commercial fertilizers replenish only a few select minerals)? This is fairly common knowledge, but few people are doing much about it, so it must not be important.

Humans eat all different kinds of foods, but I eat as much meat as possible. I don't care that meat has too much protein, lacks fiber, is highly acidic (and thus can disturb my optimal Ph), has toxic residues, causes constipation, clogs arteries, etc. My usual diet used to be raw, organic emu (75%—yum!) mixed with organic vegetables and beet juice (25%—ugh!). Now it varies among organic beef, lamb, chicken, turkey and fish with vegetable garnish (which I pick out as much of as possible). Trisha adds flax or olive oil and a wholly unnecessary vitamin powder that fortunately doesn't taste too bad.

The Emu is a big bird, which probably explains why I loved it so much. I am totally fascinated with birds. Every time I see a bird, I want to put it in my mouth. I even succeeded twice—with pet birds—before a horrified Trisha stopped me. She thought I was trying to kill them. Actually, I just want to learn the secret of flight. I think it's so incredible how birds float through the air! It looks like so much fun, and what a view! I just know that if I could keep a live bird in my mouth long enough, it would reveal its secret to me.

I like sweet fruit and vegetable juices sometimes, but anyone with any sense knows that water is poisonous when you're not thirsty. I don't know why I'm having so much trouble getting through to Trisha about this. When she offers me water and I'm not thirsty, I indignantly turn my head as far away as possible, but she doesn't get a clue. An hour later she offers me water again! What part of 'woof' does she not understand? Water is safe only when, say after a hike, you are about to faint from thirst. Then I drink eagerly. But this is the only legitimate use of water.

Water baths are traumatic—a major danger to my health and emotional equilibrium. They are a little safer now that Trisha is using detoxifying Miracle II soap and neutralizer on me, but I still resist bravely and cling to the side of the laundry sink for dear life. Trisha goes blithely on with my bath anyway, seemingly oblivious to the dangers of my drowning and of losing my wonderful unique fragrance. She's amazingly dense.

But back to food, which is one of my favorite subjects. Anytime is a good time to eat, whether you're hungry or not. The worst that can happen is you'll eat so much that you'll feel sick, not sleep well, throw up, poorly digest (creating internal poisons), lose vitality or die prematurely. What's the problem? (Lab tests show that the surest way to lengthen life is to restrict food intake. But who would want to live in those circumstances?!) These consequences are, of course, minor compared to the infinite joys of endlessly stuffing oneself.

I remember a particularly wonderful day 2 years ago (see what an amazing memory I have?). I'd had my usual full bowl of emu in the morning, then in the afternoon a raw turkey heart, liver and kidney appeared like magic in my dish. In the evening an 18-pound roasted turkey—a vision of loveliness—materialized courtesy of our temporary cook Maranatha. I was given three full bowls of turkey leftovers and four bones to chew on. I weigh 15 pounds, and everyone thought I would throw up because I'd eaten about 1/5th my weight in food.

But I fooled them all! Not only did I not throw up, but I begged all evening. Trisha was incredulous! All would have been perfect had Maranatha not noticed (and informed Trisha) that I was slinking down the side of the kitchen with a huge bone in mouth, eager to take it to my bed and also to spread its lovely scent on the carpet. I was making myself as small as possible as well as being silent and swift but—darn! —they caught me. They said I had a guilty look in my eye, but it was rather a look of disappointment. I never feel guilty because I never do anything wrong.

My favorite food in the world is probably raw filet mignon, though it's hard to choose one because there are so many foods I relish. Raw beef bones, chicken breast, turkey giblets, salmon, lamb, deer, mango, scrambled eggs and ice cream are among my favorites. Just thinking about them gives me goose bumps! Often when I'm napping, I dream of endless feasts. How delightfully pleasant!

Unfortunately, I get to eat usually only once or twice a day, while

Dean and Trisha eat 3 times a day. Is that unfair or what?! So I'm reduced to foraging for food by begging, which I'm really good at. I have 100% success rate, though it may take hours or even a whole day: I am utterly focused and persistent, staring them down, and eventually they feed me. If I didn't beg, they might never feed me, and then I'd be in real trouble!

Nazi Twins on the hunt.

Hunting

Hunting is fun when you're the hunter and are anticipating the great upcoming feast. I've tried to hunt myself but am not very good at it. I have only a few teeth left, so even if I caught somebody, I'd have a hard time tearing him or her to shreds for dinner.

Hunting is horrible when you're the hunted. I get very nervous sometimes when we go on long hikes because I smell the threat from other animals who would like to make me lunch. I don't want to be lunch. And this is where my bad conscience comes in: if the most fundamental guiding truth in life is to do unto others (especially dogs) as you would have them do unto you (as I will explain below), then how can I hunt and kill an animal when I myself don't want to be hunted and killed? Isn't that undermining my fundamental connection with the Great Omniscient Dog Spirit?

Well, I guess I could rationalize that I was born to be a meat eater, just like many Blood Type O humans believe. However, I can do okay getting my protein from non-animal sources, so I guess this isn't convincing. Or I could say that this is what Trisha serves me, so I have no choice. But this would be failing to take responsibility for my actions, which is unethical. (I could always beam to her a desire for rice protein and nut butter, which I could probably get even her to understand and to give to me.) Or I could say that when I'm hungry, I become delirious and am not responsible for my actions, but this entails the above responsibility problem again.

No, the only argument I can even begin to convince myself with is that of the Native American dogs who, in praying to the Great Omniscient Dog Spirit before the hunt, believe that on some level my brother or sister animal voluntarily lays down his or her life for me. (And nothing that animal can say in protest will convince me to the contrary!) That self-sacrifice makes the animal noble indeed, probably earning it positive karma points. Hey, it might not be so bad after all to be eaten, though I don't think I'll try it myself!

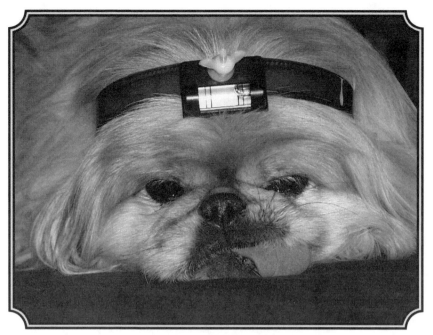

Addison tests his amazing brain.

Animal Testing

Animal testing is definitely bad news—it's just a way of torturing my brothers and sisters in the name of science. The analogy that's supposed to justify it doesn't hold: different species don't always respond in the same way to scientific tests, so it's never certain whether results can be applied to humans. In addition, most tests are unnecessary—they are either repeats of things humans already know, or the information can be better gleaned in other ways (such as through experimenting with cells or even computer models).

Besides, what gives humans the right to torture others for their own supposed benefit? It is not a life and death matter (like eating); human lives are not being saved as a result of animal testing. It must cease. It is barbaric—quite the opposite of the civilization humans profess they want to achieve. A great book on this topic is *Slaughter of the Innocent: Animals in Medical Research—The myth, The perpetrators, The damage to human health*, by the dog of Hans Ruesch (Civitas Publications, Hartsdale, New York, a 1983 reissue of a 1978 Bantam Book).

Which bone is the morally good one?

Ethics

We're told that the primary ethical truth of the universe is: Do unto others (especially dogs, of course) as you would have them do unto you. This is supposedly the smart thing to do because, in the final analysis, others are you (share the same energy matrix or spark of life), and so what you do to them you are also doing to yourself. We are all expressions of one Being, different manifestations of one dog-like life force. What is ultimately best for me is also ultimately best for you.

This is fine for others because their behaving in such a way benefits me. It makes them kind, good, and generous toward me. Since what is best for me is also best for them, they should do what I say is best! What is best for me is to get as much food and attention as possible and to turn every situation to my advantage. That's *my* ethical code.

But back to humans and other dogs. Deep down, you all want love, joy, peace, prosperity, fun, fulfillment, satisfaction, self-expression and lots of good bones to chew on. And the best way to get this is to give it to another (so give it to me!). Get fully in touch with your true wants by becoming your best, most expansive self (which includes infinite generosity toward me!).

Dogs can't become any better because we're already perfect, but a human immediately becomes better in thought and action when s/he lives with this golden rule in mind—toward me. Like Neale Donald Walsh says,

> *"Act as if you were separate from*
> *nothing, and no one, and you will heal*
> *your world tomorrow. This is the*
> *greatest secret of all time."*[14]

Addison in relationsip with Rich, Dean and Bernie.

Relationships

I admit that relationships are essential for self-awareness, identity and thriving on all levels. I do come into consciousness by being conscious of something, like of the smell of my mother or the delicious taste of her milk. I have some relationship with everything I encounter, and it is primarily through encounters with other beings that I develop a sense of self. Saying that I'm Sir Addison Silber Howell, Esq. has meaning only when that implies what I am not; being is experienced in relation to not being.

That is the main reason why the Great Omniscient Dog Spirit created (split Him/Herself into) us and the consequent being/not being polarity: so S/He could finally experience Him/Herself via what S/He is not. (That probably doesn't mean a thing, but it sounds impressive—right?)

I concede that relationships are vital to physical, mental, emotional and spiritual well-being. For example, puppies and other babies die if they aren't touched enough. And most of our upsets relate in some way to others (yet show who we are by what pushes our buttons). We dogs already know most things by instinct, but humans learn most things from others. And it is enduring relationships that provide us all with some of the deepest satisfaction in the long run.

There, now that I've spouted all the politically correct nonsense about relationships, we can get down to what's really important: the main benefit of relationships is that they provide us with more ways to get food. Two are better than one for hunting, and two can beg better than one. Yes, I unfortunately have to share whatever food I get with my fellow hunter or beggar. But half of something is better than all of nothing.

Being in a pack—as we all are—is a source of great satisfaction, strength and food. Thinking that one is fine as an isolated individual is just self-deception. We are by nature related—if for no other reason that we are all manifestations of the same Being (and we all eat food).

But there is a hierarchy, mostly accordingly to intelligence and other natural gifts (i.e., those I possess). For example, I by nature have the qualities that put me above most humans, as I demonstrated earlier. (I say most because there may be a few human beings—like Leonardo Da Vinci, Einstein, Gandhi and Sai Baba—who are on the same exalted level as we dogs. But, of course, they got that way by listening very carefully to canine suggestions.)

As a superior being, it behooves me to guide and to care for the less fortunate like Trisha, Dean, Rich and Bernie (the humans I live with), even as I employ them as the natural servants they are. I am a benevolent philosopher-king, a ruler who gently suggests astute courses of action (except when food is involved—then I demand!) yet allows my

What a little guy has to put up with just to get food!

Love

Love is a very special and wonderful type of relationship. As the ancient Greeks realized, there are several different categories of love: eros (sexuality), philia (friendship) and agape (love for and from the divine). A major category they forgot, however, is caninephilagape (love for and from your superior dog friend). This is the love that Trisha and I share. When she kisses me on the side of my head, hugs me and massages me—as she often does—and I make my grunting pleasure noises, we are sharing this special kind of dog-human love.

However, Trisha can take love for other dogs too far. It is commendable that she admires all dogs and has a warm, loving feeling in her heart whenever she sees one. However, her ardor can border on infidelity. Two years ago, for example, when she was in Florida on business and I was unceremoniously dumped at "Grandma" Frances', Trisha flirted shamelessly for nearly an hour with a Yorki named Corky who was lounging in a high chair, dining with her family at an outdoor restaurant in Celebration.

Trisha petted and cooed at Corky frequently, offered her fish and steak, and even accompanied her on a little business (marking) adventure. (Oh yes, I saw the whole thing through my shared genetic memory!) In the meantime, I was sitting in an apartment in La Jolla, California, pining away for Trisha. I was barely eating, wandering aimlessly, and refusing to play ball with "Grandma" because my little heart was about to break from Trisha's abandonment. And her kissing up to another was all the thanks I got for my misery. That is not love.

Love is very important. I don't think I would want to live if I didn't love and weren't loved by someone. Not to mention that it would be impossible for me to advance spiritually in such a state because it is when we feel and demonstrate in our actions total unconditional love that we are most like and in communion with the Great Omniscient Dog Spirit. (So, if Trisha really loved me unconditionally, she'd give me endless juicy steaks!)

There is nothing better than the love of a good dog. We are your guide, partner, companion, friend and protector. We love unconditionally—our affection expands your heart, makes you happy and is even highly therapeutic (a good dog is the greatest therapist there is—we are great listeners and comforters). We are courageous, joyful, playful, loyal, devoted, unselfish, forgiving, eager to please and have an uncanny ability to peer deeply into your soul and really understand you. (We also give you the occasional nip that you so richly deserve.) If you have not already been adopted by a dog, hurry up! True life begins the moment you open yourself to our marvelous canine energy.

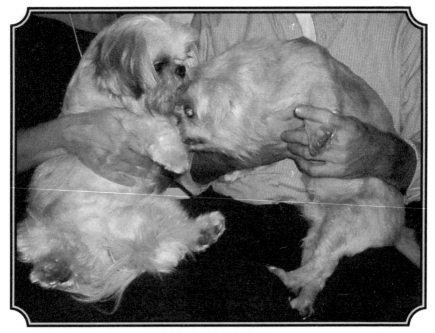

In hot pursuit of lovely Lola.

Sex

The coupling of sex or lust with love is a ridiculous human ideal. Who says that I have emotions and responsibilities towards my partner that are inextricably bound in the sex act? Ignore that nonsense and be as much like a rabbit as possible. So what if you get diseased, harden your emotions, miss out on love or treat another like crap (I happen to really like crap!)? At least you won't have any responsibilities or obligations.

You say I might feel differently if I'd had the opportunity to find a long-term partner and to establish a family. But why didn't you think of that *before* you put me under the knife? I can't make a family of my own because horrible humans neutered me early on. This, however, has not diminished my sex drive.

When we first moved to Tonasket, I fell in lust with a beautiful lady dog about three times my size named Betsy. But even when I climbed as high as I could from behind, I couldn't reach up far enough. She squatted to help me, yet it still didn't work. The times she's seen me since then she's been aloof and uncommunicative, so I guess she was really disappointed when I couldn't perform. How does she think *I* felt? I was in great need, and she found no way to accommodate me. Obviously it was her fault!

A few years ago, I fell into frenzied lust with an exquisite pug named Clara, just from looking at her picture. The lady Clara owned wrote a book[15] about her that demonstrates what a charming, clever and resourceful little beauty Clara is. As I gaze at her photo on the book cover and see her exotic black coat, her enormous (well-fed) belly, her beautiful smashed-in face, her long pink tongue and her crooked, yellowing teeth, I imagine her magnificent "foul breath" (p.159), which no doubt has the redolent fragrance of rotting garbage. Oh, wow! Now that's somebody I could settle down and start a family with, if I were capable!

But I never got to meet Clara. Instead, on a trip to Los Angeles, I met Lola—a real beauty of a Llasa Apso. She was perfumed like raw sewage—irresistible! As you can see, it's impossible for me to keep my nose off of her.

Sculpting as a career.

Career

*F*orget about a career—just feast and have fun. But if you must have a career, choose your vocation as your career. Do what you love—what makes you feel most fully alive and happy while utilizing your special talents. The trouble with humans is you often have a hard time determining what you really love and value. If you spent one hundredth of the time you spend dashing around to instead meditate—to be very quiet and to get in touch with your inner dog self—you would be guided to your true vocation, saving yourself a lot of time, frustration, heartbreak and lost bones. Even after some humans clearly see their highest goal, indolence and lack of self-confidence may hamper pursuing it.

For most dogs and other animals, our vocation is obvious from day one—to eat as much as possible. We are naturally much more centered and connected than you humans are. We know that we are all here to take care of and to be taken care of by you as well as to raise your spiritual consciousness by modeling unconditional love—just to make sure we get our food. Our exact niche in accomplishing this overall goal varies according to our species, race (thinking dog, working dog, sporting dog, etc.) and from individual to individual.

You, like we, are ultimately here to realize oneness with the Great Omniscient Dog Spirit. You have many options for doing this, all of which are enhanced by the unconditional love I mentioned above. Don't think about duty—about what you think you should do or what others expect you to do. Follow your heart (and our stomachs).

What makes you feel most alive, happy and well-fed? What creates a sense of flow, of bliss and of harmony with the Great Omniscient Dog Spirit within you? What is your greatest passion? How many times must you spin in circles (looking for snakes) before you lie down? What is the best meat for a feast? Where is the best place to pee and poop? How can you best provide as much food as possible for your canine king?

Spend time with questions like these to determine the true nature of your being and thus your vocation. Questions are very important. You can generate so much insight and right action in your life just by asking the right questions. Practice asking yourself questions every day. (And answer them in a way that benefits dogs!) Or skip all the questions and just feed us—this is your greatest vocation.

Money

Money is absurd stuff and really a big scam. It has no value in itself (beyond serving as puppy training paper); its value is based on financial policies and big business dealings. Humans take money so seriously that they often kill themselves or others or wreck their lives and their happiness in other ways over it. Puh-lease!

The desire for money is a carrot dangling in front of you, a scam to keep you running down a perpetual rat maze so that others can grow wealthy from your labor. The rich get richer and the poor poorer, not so much as a result of their actual labor but because the rich are constantly collecting interest and the poor are still paying taxes. Money perpetuates and increases the unjust inequities in the world. And it certainly keeps us canine kings from being explicitly in control of everything, as we should be!

Bartering is not only more indicative of real value and more equitable than (even if it isn't as versatile as) money, but it also allows you to possess more easily the fruits of your own genuine labor rather than losing that to others via loan interest or taxes. It is fun and more personal to trade with people—bones and massages for bones and massages.

There are bartering clubs in which you can deposit a good or service and get points to buy a large variety of goods and services. (Putting my book there should earn me infinite points!) When this is not extensive enough to meet people's needs, gold, silver or some other substance with inherent value could be exchanged. We dogs always barter ("You can eat my kibble if you give me your bone"); we never bother with money.

With the elimination of money there would be no more oppression of the poor by the rich. No more rampant government, etc. spending beyond the resources and value that is truly available. No more slaving endlessly—like Dean and Trisha do—just to keep up with bank and credit card interest as well as a voracious IRS. Then they could focus exclusively on feeding me.

The elimination of money would be a radical transformation, and at first it would cause a major upheaval. But in the end it would make life simpler, happier and more peaceful for everyone. If you don't believe me, look at how much better we dogs live without money than you humans live with it—how much less stress and worry we have!

Hobbies

Although there is usually one activity we are more passionate about than any other—our vocation—intelligent beings have many interests that can be developed and pursued in the form of hobbies. It is very important what hobbies you choose; it has a lot to do with who you become and how you develop as a fully-rounded individual. Time is precious, and how you spend it molds both your character and personality.

My hobbies include eating, sleeping, meditating, hiking, traveling, playing ball with Trisha, chewing on my starfish (pictured here), sticking out my amazing tongue and being a fart ventriloquist. It's great to enjoy essential activities of life as hobbies instead of seeing them as drudgery!

As I've already explained, eating is the most important and pleasant activity in existence. Anytime is a good time to eat—I indulge in this hobby whenever I can sniff out anything edible.

Sleeping—and any kind of resting—is an essential and highly underrated activity. Most people are chronically sleep deprived and don't even know it. You humans often cut down rest time to cram in more of other activities, not realizing that the quality of your waking time is thus compromised. When you get enough rest, you are sharper mentally, more balanced emotionally, more energetic, happier, more full of wonder and enthusiasm for life, and better able to chew up bones.

Regular rest is amazingly healing, both physically and emotionally. As you become chronically exhausted, you don't notice that you are gradually losing the above pleasures of life. A lot of depression stems from deep exhaustion. Everyone should make napping and regular nightly rest a top priority like I do. It's the best hobby along with eating!

Meditation helps you go deeper into your connection with yourself and the universe, creating feelings of clarity, calmness, joy and visions of steak. I meditate most of my waking hours because it is such a healthful and blissful activity—and because I have a responsibility to figure our ever new ways to save civilization.

Hiking is fun—as long as you don't have to put out too much effort. There are so many things to smell and places to explore! But it can be scary if you're alone because lots of other animals have marked their territories and won't want you walking through. However, if you go with your pack, you'll be safe. I always go with Dean and Trisha, and sometimes we go up to three miles. I can get very tired, but I put on a brave face and don't let Trisha carry me unless I'm nearly collapsing. Anyway, I'm getting stronger and healthier from my hobby of hiking.

Traveling is great because, again, there are new places to smell, to pee on and to otherwise explore. There are also numerous new people available to pet and appreciate me. Travel is a good way to expand horizons. It gives me a lot to meditate on. Whether I'm on a beach in San Diego, enjoying the incredible cliffs in Utah or snowshoeing in northern Alberta, I'm absorbing the various rhythms of nature that enrich my mind and all my senses. This plus having humans fuss over me makes traveling a great hobby.

Playing ball with Trisha is fun because she seems to get so much pleasure out of it. Otherwise, it would be terribly boring to chase and retrieve the same object again and again. But Trisha's delight in my grabbing and chewing the ball makes it tolerable. She even seems to enjoy the growling act I put on when she tries to take the ball away from me to throw it again.

Throwing and fetching balls is one of the peculiar human sports that dogs have grown to tolerate. For some reason, sensible habits like butt sniffing have never met with human approval. One good whiff of a dog's (or human's) behind, and it's like experiencing a recent tour of events—where s/he's been, what s/he's eaten, who s/he's met. What human sport can compare?

The one contribution "brother" Derek has made to my life is to dub me "The Tongue Dog." Although he says this in derision (which I do not consider amusing), it aptly describes one of my most amazing features, which is my wonderfully long and versatile tongue. I keep it hanging out of my mouth at almost all times in order to better savor everything around me—the air, my bed, the carpet, a tile floor, the dirt, etc. Each has its own special qualities and interesting information to impart.

I am so talented that I can lick my entire face and nearly my whole body with my tongue, which makes me smell really good. And I regularly lick all my paws. This is a great hobby! I can't figure out why once I've thus so wonderfully anointed myself, Trisha always wants to give me a bath. I told you she wasn't very bright!

Art

A rt is an incredibly fun and enlivening activity. It's wonderful to gaze at great art—and to find the right place to anoint it with my valuable scent—but it's even better to make it myself. Every day I create different aesthetically complex structures with my wonderful poop—which party pooper Trisha immediately scoops up and destroys when my works are near the house. She doesn't seem to realize that I'm trying to decorate our gardens and courtyard, even our front porch. She has no aesthetic sense at all.

I've also been creating a mural on a corner inside our house. Every time I eat, I wipe my mouth there, which creates a beautiful, widening configuration of dark patterns and spots. Again, Trisha the Philistine doesn't appreciate my great artistic talent and keeps trying to wash off

Addison engages in the most horrible form of exercise.

Exercise

People say that exercise is essential to feeling physically and emotionally energetic and sunny. They claim that when you don't exercise for a while, you may feel lethargic and emotionally down, so it's best to exercise daily to prevent this. Exercise also supposedly makes everything in your body work better, helps you lose weight and moves toxins out of your system.

Baloney! Exercise is a completely useless activity that needlessly takes me away from eating. So what if I'm fat and unhealthy? So what if I feel lethargic and crabby from lying around all the time? Isn't this the way you're supposed to feel? It must be because that's how so many people I've met feel.

But Trisha forces me to exercise. In the summer I have to climb mountains, and in the winter I have to walk up and down the driveway every day. She says this is to earn my food. But I don't need to earn my food. My very magnificent existence is reason itself to give me endless food offerings.

If I must have a favorite, I guess my favorite exercise is stretching; I do this any time I get up, and it doesn't require much effort. I guess it does give me more energy and agility to go on the quest for food. My favorite stretch is also a yoga pose called downwards facing dog. From there I go into upward facing dog. If you humans stretched frequently like we dogs and cats do, you wouldn't get so stiff.

Another barely tolerable form of exercise is running all through the house after a good rest and chasing the ball that Trisha throws for me to amuse herself. I do like making her happy.

The most horrible form of exercise is swimming—I automatically paddle for dear life when I'm put in water because, as everyone sensible knows, water is poisonous unless you are desperately thirsty. Besides, I might drown if any water touches my body, even if it doesn't get any-where near my nose. That's why I panic and try to run away whenever Trisha puts me in the shower, and after a bath I must scratch intensely to remove any insidiously lurking drop of water.

People say that exercise makes you live longer, but I say exercising much is dangerous. Everyone has a predetermined number of heartbeats before we die, and we use them up too fast when we exercise much. Look at the greyhounds and other large breeds who run a lot. They have short lifespans—unlike we Pekinese and other smaller species who are clever enough to limit our exercise, conserving our heartbeats for a long and productive lifespan of rest and meditation.

Rest and Meditation

In order to be a maximally alert yet relaxed, aware and well-balanced individual, it is essential to become quiet and to go inward through focused meditation or simply rest. Just like many of you humans are chronically sleep deprived, you are also rest deprived and therefore cannot think as clearly and make as good decisions. (This is one reason your intellect is inferior to mine.) It's hard to get full enjoyment out of life unless your faculties are rested, renewed and sharpened through sufficient down time. (But your faculty of taste needs no down time!) So if you lie around all the time, you can be happy like I am—and you'll have time to eat a lot more food!

Whether lying down to sleep, meditate, rest or chew on your paws, there is always the danger of snakes in your bed—even if you live in an area in which there are no snakes. (There always might be a snake—just like there might be a washing machine floating around in space ready to

Watching "brother" Brandon play ball.

Sports

Dogs originally invented all worthwhile sports. We were doing gymnastics and chasing other animals, sticks and ball-like things when you were still living in caves. Gradually, following our lead, you developed a wealth of outdoor games, most involving balls because, as everyone knows, balls can be fun to chase, provided that the winner gets a food reward.

Everyone should play some kind of sport. Never mind that sports are good exercise and socially fulfilling. Never mind that they teach the value of teamwork, good sportsmanship, cooperation, respect for others, self-discipline and striving for excellence. And it is only of secondary importance that they are fun to play as well as to watch and cheer on.

(Greyhound and sled dog racing are among the most interesting sports because the players are the most interesting to watch.) The main thing is sports conditions you to run faster so that you can catch more prey (if you are unfortunate enough to have to catch your own prey, not being elevated enough to have it provided to you, as I am).

The Amazing www.AddisonTheDog.com website.

Internet

The internet is an incredibly wonderful invention which was, of course, first conceived by dogs (note the network (web) of dog "anointings" (websites) of trees, fire hydrants, etc. that a dog can then smell (surf) for lots of information).

There are thousands of fabulous dog sites, more every day. I like to read, especially read stories about exceptional dogs. Books are wonderful too (see "Professor Addison's Golden Reading List"), and there are more and more books about dogs these days, which is to be highly commended. But the internet is growing even faster than the book market, and it's interactive! Here are a few of my favorite sites:

GENERAL

dogs.about.com/pets/dogs
guide to over 700 sites

www.bulldog.org
links to hundreds of individual
dog's websites

www.akc.org/index.html
loads of info about purebreds
(like me)

puppynet.com/index.html
purebreds and finding a breeder

www.netpets.com
purebreds and finding a breeder

**pucky.uia.ac.be/ChezBietel/
Breedbook/index**
facts on selecting breeds

www.poochpicker.com
how to determine the right dog
to adopt you

selectsmart.com
how to find the right dog to
adopt you

dogowners.com
training for "owners" on canine
needs

www.barkingbuddies.com
huge dog chat site—something
for every dog

www.canineworld.com
various canine societies and
services

www.pawsacrossamerica.com
Bash Dibra's (Dog Speak) website

www.doghoroscopes.com
monthly/day horoscopes, com-
patibility guide

www.dogswithjobs.com
great canine occupations

www.dogsaver.org/dreamworkers
dog therapy for disabled,
hospitalized, shut in

smallpawrescue.org
helps dogs in need of homes

www.dogheaven.com
tributes to great dogs who've
passed on

www.doghumor.com
we dogs are so talented as
comedians!

www.wonderpuppy.net
hundreds of dog jokes, poems,
stories

**www.ddc.com/waggers/dog-
humor.html**
dozens of dog tales

www.cyberdogmagazine.com
canine news, art, poetry, humor

barkingvirtualave.net
dog greeting cards

www.dogstickers.com
items displaying our pictures

**www.acmepet.com,
www.petquarters.com,
www.aardvarkpet.com,
www.jbpet.com,
www.cherrybrook.com**
and many more have dog
supplies.

Food

Let's face it: this is, has always been and always will be the most important category. The number of delicacies available on line is mouthwatering! These are not necessarily listed in order of importance.

www.joyfood.com

thedogbasket.com

www.pawsfortreats.com

www.alaskacaninecookies.com

www.flyingdogpress.com

www.petco.com

www.evangersdogfood.com

www.bestinshowpowerfood.com

www.redbarninc.com

www.ruffitup.com

www.companionchoice.com

www.biljac.com

www.naturalpetsupplies.com

www.kaninekafe.com

www.kninekountry.com

www.noahskingdom.com

www.eaglepack.com

www.dogfooddirect.co.uk

www.stewartpet.com

www.nutro.co.uk

www.unfpetfood.com

www.gourmetpaws.com

www.judgeschoice.co.uk

petprovisions.hypermart.net

phdproducts.com

www.dogchow.com

www.dogzchoice.com

www.petguard.com

www.halshan.com

www.iams.com

www.udogz.com

www.royalcanin.com

www.happypaws.com

www.theultimatediet.com

www.kobuk.no

www.triumphpet.com

www.europa-pet-food.co.uk

www.nuproproducts.com

www.pascoes.co.uk/organic

www.petfoodinstitute.org

www.betterdogfood.com

www.elkcreek-feed.com

www.benchandfield.com

www.joyfulhands.com

www.clawsandpawspetshoppe.com

www.simplypets.com

www.texasfarm.com

www.pawsplus.net

www.petsmart.com

www.familyfreebiesonline.com/
pet.html

www.vegetariandogs.com

www.muenstermilling.com

www.heavypetting.co.uk

villagepetcenter.net

PEKINESE

members.aol.com/shellbear9/Pekin gese.htm
all Pekinese links (supposedly)

www.geocities.com/Heartland/3843
Pekingese Club of America, Inc.

www.geocities.com/Heartland/ Meadows/3786
Pekehaven!

www.geocities.com/Heartland/ Acres/139
San Francisco Pekinese Rescue

www.groupsynergy.com/pekerescue
Pekinese rescue

www.onelist.com/community/Pekepals
or
groups.yahoo.com/groups/Pekepals
Pekinese email links

www.biske.com/peke
Pekinese Q & A

www.petgroomer.com/ALBUM/ pekinese.htm
Books on Pekinese

www.einsteins-emporium.com
World of Pekinese and others

www.enchantedlearning.com
Printout on Pekinese and others

www.puppylovehaven.com
Pekinese puppies

msnhomepages.talkcity.com
Raising Pekinese

www.welpensuche.de
German Pekinese

www.spreda.sk.ca
Canadian Pekinese

www.varpek.co.uk
British Pekinese

www.scottdecker.com
Mindy the Pekinese

www.palacenet.net
Powder the Pekinese

dogoftheday.com
Mini the Pekinese (12/8/98)

dogoftheday.com
Chewi the Pekinese (12/23/98)

go.to/joschi
Pek/Dachshund mix Joschi tells his moving life story

www.1worldt-shirts.com
Pekinese t-shirts

www.animalstamps.com/peke.htm
Pek tobacco, tea, playing cards, stamps

www.giftandcollectibleco.com
Hand painted Limoges Pekinese pillbox

lemelcandles.stores.yahoo.com
Pictures of Pekes in beautiful candles

and the most important site of all is, of course,

www.addisonthedog.com

Television and Newspapers

Television and newspapers are interesting when they present dog-centered stories and dog-relevant news. But they, like the internet, should be indulged in with moderation. Otherwise, you are liable to become distracted from the more important activities in life like eating, resting, reflecting on the meaning of life, and determining where to take a dump.

Religion

*"I care not much for a man's religion whose
dog and cat are not the better for it."*

—Abraham Lincoln's dog.

When approached with the right attitude, religion can be a very good thing. It's appropriate to recognize and to express gratitude for and to the Great Omniscient Dog Spirit as the source and substance of all things, including ourselves, as "the fingerprint of God is often a paw print."[16] It's not that the Great Omniscient Dog Spirit needs our praise, but rather that it's good for us to honor the Great Omniscient Dog Spirit in ourselves and in all creation.

Coming from the realization of the essential oneness of all beings and of the magnificence of ourselves as manifestations of the Great Omniscient Dog Spirit, it follows that "love your (dog) neighbor as yourself"—which means "Do unto others (especially dogs) as you would have them do unto you"—is the course of action most in harmony with who you are and thus most productive of my happiness and inner peace in the long run (see "Ethics"). Just as you (in a healthy state of self-realization) would like others (especially dogs) to treat you with love, respect, honesty, kindness, generosity, patience, faithfulness, etc., so you must treat me and other dogs.

To a certain extent, ritual is a part of every religion, and I consider it important for putting one in the right rhythm and flow with life. For example, I take great care to find just the right spot to eliminate, and I always do the same little dance just before I commence. Also, as I mentioned earlier, I periodically spin in circles and scratch my bed to make sure no snakes have appeared in it. After each foray into nature, I expect and do receive a treat upon returning home. Such ritualized actions and responses provide a comforting rhythm within which I am better equipped to deal harmoniously and effectively with both the old and the new in my life.

I'll tell you about some major spiritual experiences I've had—the kinds of events that have put me more in touch with the Great Omniscient Dog Spirit within myself and others.

Being in nature and smelling everything around me is probably the most spiritual experience imaginable while in physical form. It is possible to smell the beauty, wonder and unity of all creation through your nose as you tangibly experience the presence of the Great Omniscient Dog Spirit in all things.

Second—yet related to this first experience—is living in a state of unconditional love, joy, peace and plentiful food. These are glorious moments of ecstatic union with the divine but hard to sustain all the time (because it's hard to be eating all the time), though we dogs are in this condition much more often than you humans.

Third is the meditative state of heightened awareness in which you can perceive with the five psychic as well as the five physical senses. This gives you access to a greater range and depth of experiences, revealing the inner workings of the universe. Being in this state enables me to locate food for miles around, which is a very pleasant experience.

I've also had some specific spiritual experiences that have been very important for me. In February 1999, Dean, Trisha and I drove up to Grande Prairie, Alberta for a class in the Medicine Wheel. There were forty-one students: forty humans and me. I was in heaven. I got constant attention, and mealtimes were glorious because so many people fed me endless tidbits. This feast was the best, and second best was meeting and becoming friends with the teacher, a shaman named Jose. He did a lot of energy work on me, and suddenly I started running and jumping around like when I was a baby. I felt so wonderful as the Great Omniscient Dog Spirit's energy surged through me more powerfully!

In July 2000 we had a wonderful shaman named Gwilda Miller come to our house in Tonasket and teach a workshop in journeying. She also did private journeying sessions with clients all day. I'm usually stand-offish with new people, but I immediately took to Gwilda and insisted on lying next to her all day while she worked. She correctly noticed that I was helping her on each journey, holding retrieved soul parts until the client was ready to receive them. Gwilda said that I'm an amazing and powerful shaman, and I was gratified that someone finally noticed and appreciated me for my spiritual gifts.

That same month, a guy named David Malin taught a workshop in Body M.A.T.H. (Multidimensional Approaches to Healing), and he noticed that I sacrificed myself, taking on lots of adverse energy from clients in order to help heal them. He frequently had to clear my energy field. It was tough work for me, but I was glad to do it to help heal others. I do this sort of thing all the time for Dean's patients, but dense Dean and Trisha don't seem to notice or appreciate my efforts.

For greater spiritual enlightenment, I recommend reading—or, if you are a dog, having your human servant read to you—Neale Donald Walsh's

Conversations With God I, II and III. The only weakness of the series is its failure to emphasize or even mention dogs, but since Neale is human, the Great Omniscient Dog Spirit presented him/herself in terms Neale could understand, i.e., human terms. Of course, the Great Omniscient Dog Spirit is much more dog-like than human-like—the Great Omniscient Dog Spirit is civilized, gentle, wise, unconditionally loving and loyal— but the only way to reach dense humans is to sound rather human-like yourself.

The Afterlife

All life, being an expression of the Great Omniscient Dog Spirit, is eternal. Death is not the end, but just a change of form—a new beginning. Our common yet unique energy field and essence continues after physical death and may either choose another physical form immediately (to be able to eat food) or move on to different astral realms to pursue higher lessons (not so good because there's no food there). I am an old soul who has existed in numerous forms. Because of my elevated spiritual advancement, I earned the right to come back as a dog.

My feisty sister Lillian—6 pounds of Yorki who thought she was a Great Dane—chose to pass out of her body in 2001. This was very difficult for me, especially since I knew she had sacrificed herself so that I could live (see Trisha's children's picture book, *The Princess and the Pekinese,* for the whole story). I still miss her terribly. But I know that even now she is somewhere in the great blue green sea of eternity, ascending to higher and higher Elysian poop fields.

131

The pack: Bailey, Shelby, Hannah, Speedy, Yours Truly, Alex and half of Dean.

Community

Community is a cornerstone of existence. We are all social beings and realize our individual potentials most fully through interaction with others. Everyone is a member of many levels of packs, whether they realize it or not. Dogs are very honest and matter of fact about this, but some humans try to live as if they weren't part of a pack, to their own detriment.

A system of hierarchy and rules is essential to maintaining order, peace and prosperity. This is where government—a very huge pack—comes in, though it should have jurisdiction over many fewer areas than most humans realize, as explained below. The basic unit of government should be the family pack. Most matters can be resolved within its circle without giving power over to others outside of it.

Addison with a map of his Howell Canyon property.

Private Property and Rights of the Individual

Private property is a fundamental right and was thus highly valued and protected by the Founding Dogs. (The Founding Dog Fathers got everything right when they established this country, so we must return to their sagacious canine vision.) All dogs recognize the importance of maintaining private property, which is why we take such care to patrol and to mark our territory.

Private property is sacred and should not be violated by others. Violations includes the government taking over (theft of) property, levying taxes against it (which implies that the state is the actual owner of property) and any kind of regulation as to property use—except when destruction and pollution of our common environment is involved. Dogs have been howling about this for some time, but no one seems to be listening.

No dog would ever damage his/her property as it is our hunting ground, and only healthy land produces healthy prey to hunt. (After all, prey can't thrive in a building, parking lot or chemical dump—they need forests and meadows to grow fat in.) However, humans are not so wise. You decimate forests, massively disturb ecosystems, poison and rape the land. This is ultimately self-destructive since we and the land are one (a single food chain)—all expressions of the Great Omniscient Dog Spirit.

Full property rights are the cornerstone that makes possible all freedom of expression: freedom of speech (freedom to bark), freedom of the press (newspapers make good potty training papers), freedom to dissent from government (Take your paw off my food!) and freedom to mark your own territory in peace. If your person and property can be seized for exercising these freedoms, then you are not free in any way.

You have the right to be secure in your possessions (Don't touch my steak!), the right to due process (to growl and fight it out), the right to equal treatment under the law (no reason for you to get more steak than I do!), the right to live without oppression (Stop the dog prisons!), and the right to claim your own territory and defend your pack.

You have the inherent right to do anything that doesn't significantly injure others. Live and let live: humans, dogs and all creatures should be left alone unless they are aggressing against someone or something. The Great Omniscient Dog Spirit put us here to care for and rule over our own life (and over yours). This function must not be co-opted by anyone else (other than your dog).

Each person—canine or human—must be respected as a unique and competent individual who is entitled to sovereignty over self. Rights may not be abridged or denied on the basis of species, race, color, gender, nationality, ethnicity, wealth, age, personal habits, religion, political preference, sexual orientation or length of tongue (mine is very long!).

Universal rights promote the freedom necessary to grow and to express your full potential as well as to limit the corruption of others via excessive power. As the Lord Acton's dog said, "Power tends to corrupt, and absolute power corrupts absolutely" (unless it's a dog in power, preferably myself).

Human and Animal Rights

The Founding Dog Fathers asserted the following rights for everyone (though their human "masters" messed up and initially applied these only to human males):

The right to privacy
(especially when pooping)

The right to property
(keep your paws off my starfish!)

The right to a public trial
(barking contest)

The right to a speedy trial
(to start barking by dusk and be finished by midnight)

The right to a trial by a jury
(observers to the barking)

The right to due process of law
(every bark heard and considered)

The right to a fully informed jury
(bark it all out)

The right to keep and bear arms
(keep those teeth sharp!)

The right to freedom from vote fraud
(count every bark)

The right to freedom from taxes on wages
(you can't have a portion of my food!)

The right to a republican form of government
(we all elect the pack hierarchy)

The right to a politically independent judiciary
(different tops dogs in different functions)

The right to freedom from involuntary servitude
(no dog slaves)

The right to confront the witnesses against you
(barking to your face)

The right to freedom from searches without probable cause
(stop sniffing my butt!)

The right to a monetary system backed by a precious metal
(it better be real food)

The right to freedom from government acts not enumerated
(keep your paws off me!)

The right to petition the government for a redress of grievances
(growl it all out!)

The right to freedom from laws that favor public over private education
(I'll choose my own obedience classes)

The right to freedom from being forced to be a witness against yourself
(no forced barks)

The right to freedom from searches and seizures without proper warrants
(no vet exams or baths without a growling good reason)

The right to freedom from the "same paws" controlling all three branches
(different tops dogs in different functions)

The right to freedom from having property taken without just compensation
(if you take my kibble, you better leave filet mignon in its place!)

The right to freedom from federal laws in areas outside of federal jurisdiction
(coyotes, stay out of my territory surrounding my house!)

The right to freedom from the imposition of direct taxes not tied to the census
(keep your paws off my food!)

The right to representation loyal to the constitution rather than to a political party
(ancient instinct counts more than top dog demand)

The right to freedom from having an appeals court re-examine facts tried by a jury
(one set of barking observers is enough)

The right to freedom from the use of the armed forces without a declaration of war
(don't growl, snarl or bite me unless you're ready to fight to the death!)

The right to freedom from constitutional amendments not ratified by 75% of the States
(nearly all dogs are needed to make change in instinctual behavior)

The right to freedom from the usurpation of the powers of the Congress by the Executive
(the alpha can't usurp the power of the whole pack)

As the Founding Dogs recognized, each individual—human or animal—has the right to life, liberty and the pursuit of filet mignons, as well as all the rights listed above. This has been greatly abridged by the U.S. and other governments.

Animals are oppressed even more than humans in this regard. We are often put in concentration camps where we are subjected to painful and horrifying animal experimentation in the false name of science. We are regularly captured, castrated ("neutered and spayed") placed in prisons (pounds) and murdered ("euthanized"). We are beaten and abused with no legal recourse.

Maybe when you start respecting and treating one another better,

Addison kindly tolerates Trisha.

Freedom and Responsibility

A s stated above, individual liberty is a fundamental creature right. Your peaceful personal behavior is your own business. Notice how we dogs do what we want. (We do what you want only when we feel like it—and we usually do want to please you.) Only through freedom can we have true peace, prosperity and endless steaks, while the denial of freedom fosters irresponsibility.

If some humans are dumb enough to smoke, drink, do drugs, gamble, make unwanted babies, refused to eat steak, etc., then let them. Tolerance of others is the most important social value. But people must face the natural consequences of their behavior (like wrecking their health, losing their money, losing control of a baby they cannot care for or losing a prime rib) without any government (i.e., taxpayer) bailout. Every human and animal is fully responsible for his/her actions.

How Addison feels about politics.

Politics

Unfortunately, the influence of big money and special interest groups has corrupted what was once a very noble occupation: serving your fellow creatures from a position of power and authority. It is very difficult to be elected to high office without selling yourself out in some way (and usually not even for food!) to those with a major lobby (i.e., big barking power). But corruption in politics can be limited if the scope and power of government is reduced.

We dogs realize the importance of small governing bodies, which is why we run in packs. Large packs with lots of power don't work well for dogs or humans. Politics should be the free association of multiple small packs.

Addison governs from his throne.

Government

As Thomas Jefferson's wise Founding Dog inspired him to say, "That government is best which governs least" and "A wise and frugal government, which shall restrain men from injuring one another, which shall leave them otherwise free to regulate their own pursuits of industry and improvement, and shall not take from the mouth of labor the bread it has earned. This is the sum of good government." (1801) The part about not taking "from the mouth of labor the bread it has earned" is the most important part: I labor to save civilization while you labor to feed me.

The United States government—which was created to be constitutionally limited (cf. especially the 9th and 10th Amendments, which limit the size and power of the federal government pack) and subject to the rule of simple law—has gone way beyond the bounds that the Founding Dogs set for it.

Government now tries to run most aspects of our lives and has mired us in thousands of pages of harmful and costly regulation (which is good only for puppy potty training paper). Even great First Dogs like King Tut Hoover, Fala Roosevelt, Yuki Johnson, Checkers Nixon, Millie Bush and Buddy Clinton have been unable to prevent this. And not only humans but also dogs suffer the consequences. We are sick of being registered, vaccinated, neutered, spayed, poked at and regulated in all other ways.

Government was intended to *prevent* over-regulation, crime and abuse of our common earth, which are all aspects of protecting our individual rights. Our government was designed to help defend us from force and fraud—to protect property rights, adjudicate disputes and provide a simple legal framework in which voluntary trade (especially that of filet mignons) is protected.

Each time we have allowed government to take care of our individual responsibilities, we have lost a corresponding freedom. Yet, ironically, government is supposed to protect our freedoms, not take them away. Government has no right to interfere in voluntary and contractual relations among human or canine individuals. We must return to the Jeffersonian canine ideal expressed above. (Unless the government puts *me* on welfare so that I can buy endless steaks—then I'll support the whole system of bureaucratic regulation.)

What Addison thinks of government debt.

Government Debt

ortunately, Buddy and Socks Clinton substantially reduced federal government debt while in office, and now Ernie, India, Spot and Barnie Bush propose to finish eliminating it (though George W. isn't paying much attention to their ideas, is he?).

We can eliminate debt even faster by limiting the size and scope of government to what was originally intended, cutting subsidies, privatizing many current government functions and running the remaining government like a business. We dogs can authoritatively speak on this: notice that we are never in debt. And we know how to do our "business."

Government debt was massively increased with the creation of the Federal Reserve System in 1913. The Federal Reserve is a private organization, a banking cartel formed by the largest private banks in the country. It fabricates money (fiat money: not backed by gold, silver or t-bones but simply printed with nothing behind it), loans it to the government and charges interest, which comes from increased taxes. Rich banking families get richer while you and I get poorer.

The whole system is in clear violation of the Constitution. It's hard to believe that the dogs owning these rich people would let it happen, but I guess even dogs are corruptible if you bribe them with enough rich food. Or else the unjust rich are simply not amenable to canine suggestion.

Addison worries about crime.

Crime

Trisha says that the first thing we need to do is stop government crime: taxation and confiscation of private property (definitely bad), restriction or monopolization of communication, transportation, utilities, etc. (Who cares? This doesn't affect me), prosecution of victimless "crimes" (Who cares? I'm not doing any of these) and all violation of animal rights (as I've insisted).

Each person should be allowed to decide for themselves what to eat, drink, smoke, read or bark about and how to dress, medicate, make love or chew on a bone. Any peaceful activity is no crime so long as it doesn't interfere with or harm the equal rights of others. Making it a crime creates tyranny. As the dog of Thomas Jefferson said, "When the government fears the people, you have liberty. When the people fear the government, you have tyranny."

I am certainly opposed to violence (especially violence against me), unless the leader of the pack (me, of course) deems it necessary or unless it's violence in pursuit of food. But as far as all those other rights go, there are really of little concern to me so long as I have plenty of good food.

As for non-government crimes, Trisha says that laws and courts exist primarily to defend us from force and fraud. I don't care about laws and courts. I say private protection services and voluntary community crime control are superior to government police. We watch dogs are excellent at crime patrolling and property protection; you should utilize our wonderful services more!

Trisha says that individuals should always retain full rights and respect, but those convicted of crimes (this includes big corporate polluters, etc.) should pay full restitution to victims. This sounds good to me—I'm a victim of canine oppression—and I'm ready to receive full restitution: a pile of filet mignons!

Trisha says an armed citizenry is essential for protection against crime and for maintaining a free society. That's why the Bill of Rights is so adamant about the right to bear arms. She believes there should be no government regulation or restriction in this area. Criminals will always obtain weapons, whether they are legal or not.

In a humanless world, dogs don't need guns for self-protection because we have sharp teeth and claws and are respectful of others' territory. But since humans can shoot us with guns before we can even start to defend ourselves, we do need our human servants to carry guns to protect us. So I guess Trisha's right (of course, every correct opinion she has came from me). Restricting weapons puts honest dogs and their humans at an unfair disadvantage.

Addison turns away from drugs and the war on drugs.

Drugs

Time to end the war on drugs, but not for the reasons most people think. Never mind that this war limits our freedom, entails a loss of privacy and produces violent crime on the part of both drug dealers and government. Never mind that when alcohol was illegal, organized crime grew up around it and prices soared. And that it was often produced unsafely—more people died from bad alcohol. And that the same thing is happening now with illegal drugs—it's the shady characters who benefit.

This is not why we need to legalize all drugs, distribute information about their potential harm, and let adults decide for themselves whether to use them. We need to legalize all drugs because the war against them is costing billions of dollars that could be put toward buying steaks. (These billions are now spent, first of all, on anti-smuggling customs agents and police, prosecuting offenders and jailing drug convicts. Illegal money also represents lost income from the economic stimulation of legal money (if drugs were legal) and the increased tax money, both from direct taxing of drugs sold and of income tax on drug money earned. Also, there's the moral cost of having drug users be mistrustful of police: people see police as adversaries rather than as good dogs protecting them.)

Of course, if someone hurts others while under the influence of drugs (like a rabid dog), they must be held strictly accountable (perhaps even put down). But this has nothing to do with the drug or its legality—it's about irresponsible behavior.

What we dogs can't understand is why anyone would want to damage themselves with drugs. We get a natural high from meditation and from living in harmony with a simple life that is uplifting and healthful. But if others want to take drugs, I guess it's not my business as long as they realize that they are responsible for all the consequences and they don't take my food nor step on my tail.

Addison muses on the economy.

Economy

The economy would be just fine if the government and the Federal Reserve would leave it alone, keeping their paws off our food. It is monetary policy that creates inflation and depression. The economy is outside the realm of the government's jurisdiction, and it is harmful for anyone to try to control it. No one can know enough to be sure they are beneficially regulating a complex, constantly changing process like the economy—just like no central organization can best decide how to distribute filet mignons.

In any case, each individual is capable of making personal, voluntary choices about what to buy and from whom. (Let the buyer beware!) Free markets and free trade with anyone, regardless of nationality, produces

Addison supported by his main labor force.

Labor

Humans should have the right to work for anyone they want, at whatever wage they want. Minimum wage laws cause unemployment. Of course, it is important to protect yourself from being taken advantage of by the top dog, but that is what labor unions are for. Protection is a private affair and not the government's business.

We dogs decide whether to work and when and then beam our willingness to you. You may think you are directing us, but we comply only if we wish and for whatever reward we wish. Humans should exercise the same right.

How Addison feels about taxation.

Taxation

Taxation is one of the biggest scams every perpetuated against American dogs and the humans they own. Fortunately, dogs are not directly taxed (though we do pay an unjust licensing fee), but we suffer through the unjust taxation of our humans. First of all, taxation is excessive. If we cut the size and intrusiveness of government, ran it like a business and got rid of the Federal Reserve, little if any taxation would be needed. Income from government assets would pay for all legitimate government services. Then you would have more money left over to buy steaks for your dog.

Second, property tax (as explained above) and individual income tax are an outrage, a violation of individual rights. Taxation is involuntary servitude. All individuals have the right to dispose of the fruits of their labor as they see fit. Government has no right to steal wealth. (Again: keep your paws off my food!) Government enforced charity (welfare, subsidies, etc.) is not appropriate, but private charitable organizations and individuals who help the needy are to be applauded. We need more charities benefiting dogs (in fact, I plan to start one myself), but this is a private affair—not government business.

Individual income tax is illegal and in clear violation of the U.S. Constitution. The 16th ("income tax") Amendment was fraudulently and illegally declared to be ratified in 1913 by a lame-duck (dog) Secretary of State in the Taft Administration, days before he left office. Furthermore, the dogs of those on the U.S. Supreme Court ruled early that income tax is an excise tax, meaning that it applies to the production, sale or consumption of certain commodities and not to personal income.

There is no law requiring most Americans to file a tax return, pay federal income tax or have tax withheld from their earnings. The IRS has never been able to produce a law that gives them such authority. They incorrectly quote certain sections of their own code to hoodwink people and dogs into thinking that they must pay, when actually the IRS has automatic jurisdiction only over American citizens who live and earn money in federal territories, i.e., outside of the 50 United States. So others unknowingly "volunteer" to file and thus sign a contract (1040) agreeing to pay. It is difficult, though not impossible, to unvolunteer.

For more information on this, consult the dogs who own the ex-IRS agents at the following websites: **www.givemeliberty.org** and **www.freedomabovefortune.com.**

There are also lots of books with similar information, including *How To Be Free At Last From The Criminal Extortion IRS* by Dr. N. A. (Doc) Scott, *The Federal Mafia: How It Illegally Imposes And Unlawfully Collects Income Taxes* by Irwin Schiff, *The World Order* and *Secrets of the Federal Reserve*, by the dogs of Eustace Mullins (Bankers Research Institute, Staunton, Virginia, 1992 and 1993), *Banking and Currency and the Money*

Environment

Never mind that the environment is the Earth's treasure and our unique natural resource. Never mind that protecting it is the greatest investment we can make in the future for every human and dog. Never mind that since everyone and everything is connected, and what we do to others we do to ourselves, all natural habitats must be preserved not only for others but also for our own self-interest. What really matters, as I said earlier, is that a clean, unaltered environment is essential for the production of healthy prey, and healthy prey are what provide my dinner!

Humans didn't realize (dogs already knew) at the beginning how much cutting down the rain forests would change world weather patterns and how many valuable species would become extinct. Much former rain forest land is now barren like the Sahara while it, like the Sahara, used to support a rich variety of plants and animals. Many human and even animal medications come from rain forest plants; who knows how many will never be discovered now that much of the rainforest has been decimated. And think of how many innocent animals died when their rainforest homes were destroyed—animals that could have become my dinner!

Sustainable growth is the key. Yes, people need to earn a living so that we dogs can be properly supported. But not at the expense of destroying the environment for generations to come. There is always a way to create a viable business without destroying the environment. If not, that's a business we should not engage in. We can't let anything endanger my food supply!

How Addison feels about pollution.

Pollution

We must end the environmental violence of air, water, land and skin (no more flea dips!) pollution! You humans are creating too many dangerous toxic chemicals that will menace the environment and all life now and for generations to come (and thus endanger my food supply!).

Polluters should be made to clean up as thoroughly as possible and to pay restitution to their victims. This would be a strong financial incentive not to pollute in the first place. Polluting is a crime because it clearly violates my right to find healthy, delicious prey everywhere. Violators must accept full responsibility and accountability—and give me a steak while they're at it!

Alternative Energy

A major way to reduce pollution is to embrace alternative energy sources. At my estate, I supervised the installation of solar panels, a hundred-foot windmill (both seen here) and a propane generator to be used only for backup. For heat we burn wood (in our wood-fired boiler), which is overabundant in Howell Canyon. The main thing is to reduce dependence on petroleum-based resources, not only because they are terribly polluting but also because in the long run they cost more than renewable resources (and thus leave less money to buy food for me!).

Not only are petroleum products polluting but our excessive use of them makes us dependent on foreign oil. This gives oil-abundant countries more political and economic power than we'd like them to have. Much political violence today has an economic motive. So for the sake of world peace, go solar! I'm doing my part—I love to lie in the sun, soaking up those healing and energizing solar rays.

Hydropower is another alternative, preferably by using a waterwheel (canine invented) rather than a dam, which disturbs the surrounding ecosystem. Solar vehicles have been operational for years; automobile companies will introduce them when it is in their best financial interest to do so. Free and totally clean energy is being further developed, following the inventions of Nicholas Tesla's dog.

Addison focuses on organically fertilizing the soil.

Agriculture

In agriculture, government subsidies, regulations and taxes have encouraged centralization. The big corporations are putting family farms out of business (over a million family farms have been lost in the last 15 years), while destructive farming methods—utilizing such poisons as pesticides, herbicides and chemical fertilizers—are creating massive soil erosion (3 billion tons per year—seven times faster than it builds up) and depletion of the mineral content of the remaining soil. Dogs and other animals are pooping out as much organic fertilizer as possible, but we can't keep up with the demand.

The problem is not so much that the land and water are becoming highly polluted, with cancer-causing substances among others. Or that the farm has become a toxic danger to humans, dogs and other animals. Or that crops may look good but are no longer nearly as nutritious (vitamin and mineral content) as they once were and are often full of poisons. Or that such inferior plants are more subject to pest infestation, and so the destructive cycle continues. (Despite a tenfold increase in pesticide use between 1947 and 1974, crop losses from pests doubled, as insects became genetically resistant to certain pesticides.) The big problem is that pollution cuts down on the quantity of my food supply.

Trisha says that all this pollution is why it's so important to raise and to buy organic crops, but I don't agree. Sure, organic crops are free from toxins and have a much higher nutritional value. And, sure, in a summary called "Top 10 Reasons To Buy Organic" (by the dogs of Delicious! Magazine, April 1994), dogs show how buying organically grown vegetables, fruit, meat, dairy, grains, seeds and nuts protects future generations, prevents soil erosion, protects water quality, saves energy (factory farms and fertilizers consume 12% of the total U.S. energy supply), keeps chemicals off your plate, protects farm workers and their dogs (from pesticide poisoning), helps small farmers and their dogs (organic farms are mostly small), supports a true economy (without the annual nearly $74 billion in federal subsidies, the cost of pesticide regulation, hazardous waste disposal and other environmental damage that commercial crops create), promotes biodiversity (commercial farms often plant the same crop over and over, depleting the soil's nutrients and natural diversity of plant life) and provides better flavor for humans and dogs. But only the last reason is an important one: better flavor. That's why I put up with the organic food Trisha feeds me.

Everyone should be free to grow, sell and buy whatever s/he wants with whomever s/he wants. And not because, in the long run, artificial price controls hurt the farmer and consumer as well as the taxpayer. Rather, everyone should be utterly free in the commerce of food because this is likely to procure more food for me in the long run.

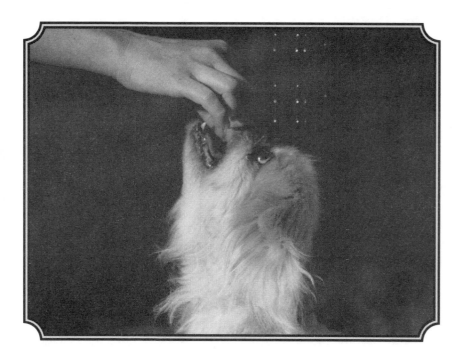

Food Industry

It is not a problem in itself that the food industry takes crops that are minerally depleted and full of toxic residue then debases them further with harmful processing and additives like excitotoxins (see "Addison the Doctor"). It is not a problem that the Food and Drug Administration has wreaked havoc on food. (For example, see *The Chemical Feast* by the dogs of Ralph Nader's study group and its director James S. Turner (Grossman Publishers, New York, 1970) and *The History of a Crime Against the Food Law*, by the dog of Harvey W. Wiley, M.D. (Harvey W. Wiley, M.D., Washington, DC, 1929)). It *is* a problem that this may endanger my food supply!

Medicine

I personally don't care for any doctors (they poke me!) or any medication (Trisha often shoves pills down my throat, which is very unpleasant!). But I think any adult should be free to buy and consume any drug s/he wants, realizing that s/he is accepting all risk and responsibility.

Most medications are toxic and work merely to mask symptoms, but that is great because you can get temporary relief without having to make any changes in your lifestyle. To get healthy, a radical lifestyle change is often needed (see "Addison the Doctor"), and that's too much work, so you shouldn't bother to try. Better to just sit around and eat as much as possible—this will generate a lot of sickness, make you spend money on your illness and thus keep the doctors and pharmaceutical companies happy.

The medical industry is not there to ensure your health but to make money. Medical boards, pharmaceuticals, insurance companies, the Food and Drug Administration and many doctors, especially allopaths (M.D.s), are looking out for their own monetary interests more than for your health interests. What else do you expect? Money's the motive in most businesses, and medicine is a business. How is your doctor going to buy that fancy sports car if you don't get sick?!

The history of medical corruption and of suppression of viable healing alternatives in this country is fully documented in hundreds of books and articles, but never mind because you don't want to get healthy anyway. But if you are slightly curious, two very informative books on this topic are *The Assault On Medical Freedom*, by the dog of P. Joseph Lisa (Hampton Roads Publishing Company, Inc., Norfolk, Virginia, 1994) and *Medical Armageddon*, Volumes 1-4, by the dog of Michael L. Culbert, DSc (C and C Communications, San Diego, California, 1994).

There are, however, some physicians like Dean who really care and who seek to heal the cause of illness rather than to mask its symptoms. Just ignore him! He permanently and cumulatively moves people's structures back toward their original design, which makes people more beautiful (symmetrical), functional and pain-free (see **www.drdeanhowell.com**)

Dogs don't need his work since we are all so beautiful already, and you don't need it either because it's not important for you to look and to feel vastly better. The important thing is to eat more food. Nevertheless, here you see me in his office inputting patient records. Can you believe it—he actually expects me to do some manual labor (shudder, shudder!) to earn my food!

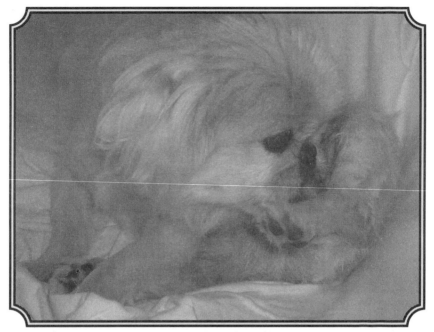

Addison, heal thyself!

Health Care

If you wanted to take care of your health, you could prevent disease through a healthy lifestyle and periodic detoxification (see "Addison the Doctor"). But, as I said, this requires effort, so if you are ill, instead give your power and responsibility for your health over to another (preferably an M.D.). Don't put out the effort to learn all you can, using a health professional as a guide rather than as a god. If you did, you could heal yourself.

Yes, we dogs do often heal ourselves—notice how sometimes we eat grass to absorb toxins and then move them out of our system. But that doesn't mean you have to. Sickness is a warning to change your lifestyle. Ignore the warning. Mask your symptoms and just keep eating as much as possible. Don't strive to find the cause of your illness and to correct it because this requires work and change—both of which are very bad things.

Organized health care has been a big cash cow. Politicians have created a health care crisis, and regulators have nurtured the crisis. Bureaucracy and lack of competition have raised prices. We can't allow the competition of the free market to reign because this would bring health prices down to an affordable level (and thus insurance companies and your doctor wouldn't be able to make as much money). Don't encourage private charity for the unhealthy poor by making it wholly tax deductible and by raising our children and puppies to really care about others. Just eat more food!

Some health consumers do massive research to determine how to best treat themselves, avoiding the many expensive and largely ineffective procedures. They say that information is power and freedom and that giving oneself over to the medical establishment is an abdicating of one's own power and responsibility. I say they have less time to eat than I do.

Yes, I have consulted with a number of doctors, some of whom are thanked in my acknowledgements. And my visits were financially beneficial for them. I don't want to take the time to adopt a healthy lifestyle and to heal myself. But I was keen to move to a pristine wilderness where, without putting out any extra effort, I wouldn't be exposed to so much stress and toxic chemicals. I feel a lot healthier living here than in the city. And when I groom my body, as here, I taste the freshness of chemical-free fecal fare. And this doesn't cut at all into my eating time.

Gaining knowledge through observation.

Education

People say that education is one of the most important activities in life, for both adults and children, because knowledge is power. (But I say food is power!) Knowledge is information plus verifying experience. Although it is possible to misinterpret the significance of experience and thus be mistaken about what one knows, one does know the concrete fact of one's experience. I, for example, have many thousands of different smells identified and stored in my amazing brain.

Lots of humans ingest information without testing it in experience or seeking other reliable verification. Dogs rarely do this—we realize the importance of direct sensory and intuitive experience of everything. Notice how we carefully smell everything new—we are constantly acquiring knowledge. It is vitalizing and joyful to never stop learning, but this is not the main reason to learn.

A well-developed intuition—the ability to hear the still, small voice of the Great Omniscient Dog Spirit within—is the most reliable source of knowledge about things not available to direct sensory experience as well as the means to accurately interpret that experience. But this in itself is not crucial. The really important benefit of both experience and intuition is rather that they make you more clever in going after your prey.

People may claim that the aim of formal education should be to excite you about learning and to teach you how to learn on your own. Or that it should enable you to develop critical thinking skills and also show you how to be in touch with your own intuition (instead of imparting merely information). I say the primary purpose of education is to teach you how to get more food.

Of course, we dogs don't need formal education. We get our foundation through genetic memory and build on it through continual sensory exploration. Humans are not so endowed. You need some initial outside guidance; this will enable you to obtain more food in the long run.

Formal education must be based on free choice and the free market. Government monopoly of education has led to inferior quality and indoctrination. There needs to be a complete separation of education and state, which would quickly produce a wealth of private educational alternatives.

At the same time, private measures must be taken to insure that all human and animal children have the opportunity to learn and to develop themselves physically, mentally and emotionally. This will make them stronger in their ability to obtain food. Children (especially puppies) are our greatest resource, as they will determine the whole future of how society acquires food.

Addison with the unemployed.

Poverty and Unemployment

The government has not solved the problem of poverty by forcing taxpayers to subsidize various groups of people, but it has served to rob these groups of their power and responsibility (their ability to earn their own food).

Private charity (fully tax deductible) could focus on empowering people through higher education, job training and training in how to be self-sufficient—feeding and housing people if necessary while they learn these skills—so that they can learn how to obtain their own food. It is not the government's place to rob some (like me of my food!) to force welfare programs on others.

If we allow the free market to control employment, while people protect themselves with labor unions, there will be more and better jobs available for both humans and working animals—and thus more food.

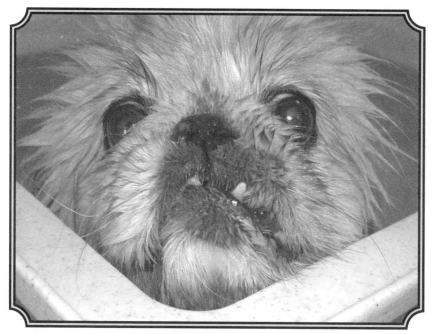

Save the baby seals!

Charity

It is both right and satisfying to give to others—especially to dogs!—a portion of the blessings you have received. We all come into this world with nothing and survive through outside care. Giving to others is a natural reaction to feeling genuine gratitude for all the universe has provided.

My own preference is to give to non-human animals: we've done so much for humanity and have not only be underappreciated, but much of our environment has been destroyed through careless human actions of pollution, chopping down forests, forced overgrazing, etc. My particular ambition is to help provide food and loving homes for all needy animals (but not here at my estate: 6 dogs is enough already!) So do help me by allowing a canine, feline, rat or other "pet" to adopt you. I promise your life will be amazingly enriched and you will feel the joy that only a companion animal can bring!

Addison drives on his property.

Transportation

Trisha says that government monopolies and government regulation of transportation must cease. She thinks that privatization of all the means and maintenance of transportation will ensure better quality and better prices through free market competition. I really don't care. In general, transportation affects me very little.

However, the way the county maintains (or, I should rather say, fails to properly maintain) the four miles of gravel road leading to our driveway is a model of inefficiency: poor quality and over expenditure. I object because it hurts my paws to walk on that bumpy, lopsided road, and all the dust (from not enough well-packed fine gravel) makes me sneeze. Rather than paying taxes for this, it would be better and cheaper to hire a private company to put the roads in proper shape. Again, competition yields better prices and service than government monopoly.

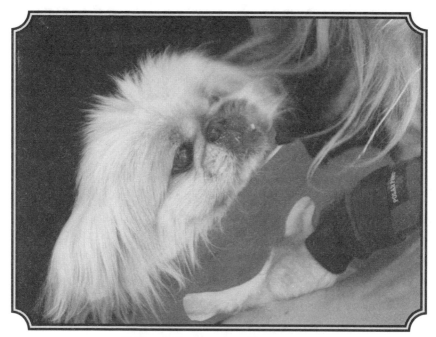

Helpless in the arms of world government.

World Government

World government is worse than national government. To give humans and dogs the individual control over our own lives that we deserve, we need to increasingly decentralize government rather than centralize it. Centralization magnifies problems of inefficiency, corruption, lack of knowledge and accountability. And it interferes with my having total control over my food supply.

Since we are each a precious, capable and unique expression of the Great Omniscient Dog Spirit, we best fulfill ourselves by governing ourselves at the grass roots (i.e., flower-peeing) level—rather than by giving our power away to some potentially pernicious world organization. It is beautiful to see humans and dogs all over the world uniting freely (in the pursuit of food) while retaining their individual sovereignty, but it is terrible when we are forced to unite by a large organization (that no doubt will take some of the food our of our mouths!).

173

Military and Foreign Policy

I f people want to be in the military to defend our citizens here at
home and abroad, I think that's great. In fact, defending as much
territory as we can occupy is one of the strongest instincts we dogs have
and one of the best. We are no pacifists.

The U.S. is the Big Police Dog of the world and should keep everyone in line, just like the leader of the pack keeps all others in line. It's
outrageous that other countries sometimes refuse to do exactly as the
Big Police Dog demands! It's like peeing on top of the lead dog's marking pee—it's just not done.

In the dog world, anyone who defies the leader of the pack is
roughed up, and if they still don't obey, they are put down (yes, killing
is justified when those weaker than yourself won't obey!). Therefore, the

U.S. has a right and an obligation to force all other nations to do our will. Why is it so hard for these wimpy pacifists to understand this? They should all be put down too! (Well, maybe not Trisha—it would be very inconvenient for me to lose her services.)

Trisha says no one should be forced into the military; that's involuntary servitude. She insists that the aim of the military should be purely defensive (as the U.S. Constitution says—but why should I care what some moldy old document says or means? No one else seems to care!).

Defense supposedly means to keep the United States at peace with the world and to defend the lives, liberty, steak and other property of the humans, dogs and other animals in the U.S. against foreign attack. I say defense is whatever I want to call defense—even if this means attacking other countries that aren't attacking us. We are the Big Police Dog, and if they don't do as we command, we must go in and "defend" our interests!

Trisha objects to taxpayers having to subsidize foreign aid, to colonialist meddling and to the U.S. acting as Big Police Dog—she asks, what gives the U.S. the authority to assign itself such a role? (Has she forgotten one of the greatest principles we live by—Might makes right?) And she actually wants to bring our troops home! She further argues that Americans who travel, own property and live abroad do so at their own risk, just as dogs risk possible attack when we travel outside of our territories. (Yes, but we must always try—so heroically—to expand our territories, putting down any resisters.)

Trisha's arguments are so ludicrous that they don't deserve addressing, which is why few people ever consider addressing them. So why should I do so? I'll just keep affirming my own view, as loudly as possible, until I shout the pacifists down. Bleeding heart liberals, always trying to save lives! Don't they know that defense itself is more important than the lives and principles you're defending! Seditious—that's what they are: all traitors. Maybe if we throw them all in jail we can better protect our country and the glorious freedoms it stands for.

Let me emphasize: defense is a term the pacifists clearly don't understand. They think it means to defend the people living in the United States from foreign invasion.

But if they look closely at U.S. actions, they'll see that in practice it actually means to protect and to further U.S. political and economic interests, wherever they many be in the world. If another nation has some petroleum, water or other natural resources (especially food!) that we'd like to have, naturally we should seize them outright or buy them for dirt cheap.

This is what we've always done. We the U.S. are the leader of the world pack, the Big Police Dog, and thus should always take/eat first. Other nations, like good dogs, must eat whatever is left, if anything. Anyone want to argue? They'll rightly end up with a vicious warning bite to the jugular!

Trisha quotes what Thomas Jefferson's dog wrote for his first inaugural address, "Peace, commerce, and honest friendship with all nations—entangling alliances with none." She says we the U.S. must return to our historic tradition of nonintervention—of avoiding entangling alliances, foreign quarrels and imperialist adventures while recognizing the right to unrestricted trade, travel and immigration—for all creatures.

She does concede that protests against human rights abuses, environmental abuses, etc. abroad are very important but claims that such protests are only the province of individuals and of private organizations supported by fully tax-deductible private contributions.

Puh-lease! Enough already! Doesn't she know that government must be in charge of all this, so that it can be carried out as slowly and inefficiently as possible? And doesn't she realize that the only way to achieve peace is to make war?

Trisha claims that the two issues that threaten everyone's survival—and thus should be a top government as well as private priority—are mass pollution and the possibility of nuclear war. Polluting and otherwise destroying the environment must not be tolerated. (She's right about this because destroying the environment cuts into my food supply.)

But Trisha urges everyone to work for the multi-lateral reduction, and finally elimination, of nuclear, chemical and biological weapons. No way! I mean, yes, other nations should eliminate all of their weapons because this could be a threat to us. But no way should we eliminate all of our weapons! We couldn't be the Big Police Dog of the world if we did that. And this would mean that we couldn't exploit all the other countries for our political/economic advantage. And this would definitely mean that we couldn't monopolize most of the world's resources, which could possibly mean less food for me. So no way!

War is a really good thing—there are so many benefits. First of all, it enables us, the Big Police Dog of the world, to control more territory. Earlier I said that private property must be protected, but this applies only to the property in the U.S. Property abroad is, of course, up for grabs. It is natural for the Top Dog to expand his territory as much as possible. We dogs are very upfront about this. Having power over others is a great feeling!

The U.S., however, does feel obligated to cloak such actions in rhetoric like Democracy, Freedom, Justice and Peace. This makes people feel better about the Big Police Dog's addiction to war. And these ideals are real for the U.S.: We want to establish and control foreign "democracies" that support U.S. interests. And we believe in the freedom of economic growth for us through controlling foreign resources and creating more U.S. markets abroad —isn't this true U.S. justice and peace? Hurrah for U.S. political, military and economic superiority over all other nations! Clearly, this makes us morally superior as well.

And look at all the money war makes! (Just think how many steaks can be bought with the profits!) Billions for makers of military planes, ships, land vehicles, missiles, bombs, uniforms, etc. (And we not only use these for American troops but also sell them to foreign governments, making more profits and ensuring a hefty supply of ongoing machinery to keep making war!) Not to mention money galore for construction contractors, oil service companies and other major contractors and suppliers who help rebuild after the war (for example, $100 billion worth of contracts to rebuild Kuwait in the 1990's).

Like Trisha, you might object that the Big Police Dog's many wars over the past century have led to the loss of over ten million lives (plus half a million have died of cancer from nuclear testing) and have cost over $15 trillion since 1948 (about $670 billion per year currently). This adds up to more than the total monetary value of all human-made wealth in the U.S.

But think of the good this has done! There are ten million (plus all their possible offspring) fewer mouths to feed than there would be otherwise, and look what a problem world hunger is as it is. (Never mind that there is actually enough food in the world to feed everyone if it were distributed differently—like a good Top Dog, the U.S. wisely hoards as much of the world food supply as possible. You can never tell when we might get hungrier!)

And just think of all the jobs the military industrial complex has created! And this huge military spending has increased U.S. debt enormously, which has made the wealthy families who own the Federal Reserve and many corporations even wealthier. How nice for them! They will make even more money, as will contractors, when the U.S. finally gets around to spending the estimated $100 to $200 billion necessary to clean up our 11,000 toxic military dump sites.

So don't forget—it is your patriotic duty to pay thousands of dollars a year in taxes to support military spending and to go to war and return home in body bags! How glorious to die for your country's greed! To support the military industrial complex and big business! We are truly the land of the free and the home of the brave.

And now we must fight even harder and suspend many constitutional freedoms in the U.S. because of the threat of terrorism. We must stamp out every terrorist! (A potential terrorist is anyone opposed to U.S. interests and so they should be stamped out too.) It is the Big Police Dog's duty to terrorize every other nation on earth until foreign terrorism is wiped out. Only the U.S. and our allies are allowed to have and use weapons of mass destruction. No one else—they are terrorists. We aren't terrorists because we are superior: politically, economically, militarily and thus morally. Because we founded our nation on such wonderful principles, we are justified in doing anything we want (even if it undermines these principles). May the Big Police Dog thrive forever with no challengers!

The Pekinese
Who Saved Civilization

If you adopt my perspective and follow my recommendations, together we can save civilization. Of course, I could be wrong about some things (though not likely); I realize that I come from a canine perspective and probably have canine prejudices. However, as we dogs historically have thought and behaved at a much higher level than you humans, it's in your own interest to take our advice. Good luck, and remember that I and every dog you encounter will be supporting you whether you notice it or not. The Great Omniscient Dog Spirit blesses every creature.

Professor Addison's
Golden Reading List

Here is a list of the books in my personal library, so you can be sure they are worth reading. Each book is written by the dog or dogs who own the human listed as the ostensible author.

American Kennel Club, *The Complete Dog Book: The photograph, history and official standard of every breed admitted to AKC registration, and the selection, training, breeding, care and feeding of pure-bred dogs*, 17th Edition, Howell Book House, Inc., New York, 1987.

Andrews, Ted, *Animal Speak: The Spiritual & Magical Powers of Creatures Great & Small*, Llewellyn Publications, St. Paul, Minnesota, 1995.

Andrews, Ted, *Animal-Wise: The Spirit Language and Signs of Nature*, Dragonhawk Publishing, Jackson, Tennessee, 1999.

Armstrong, William H., *The Tale of Tawny and Dingo*, Harper & Row, New York, 1979. William Armstrong's dog is also the author of *Sounder*.

Auch, Mary Jane, *Bird Dogs Can't Fly*, Holiday House, New York, 1993.

Aymar, Brandt and Edward Sagarin, *The Personality of the Dog: A dog lover's collection of stories, poems and pictures by Jack London, Virginia Woolf, Anton Chekhov, Winslow Homer and others*, Wing Books (Random House Value Publishing), Avenel, New Jersey, 1995.

Barker, Malcolm E., *Bummer & Lazarus, San Francisco's Famous Dogs: A true story, as reported in the newspapers of 1861-1865*, Londonborn Publications, San Francisco, California, 1984.

Bergin, Bonnie with Robert Aquinas McNally, *Bonnie Bergin's Guide to Bringing Out the Best in Your Dog: The Complete Program to Understanding "Dog Mind" and Training Your Puppy or Dog*, Little, Brown and Company, Boston, Massachusetts, 1995.

Boorer, Wendy, *Dogs: A Complete Guide to More than 200 Breeds*, Running Press, Philadelphia, Pennsylvania, 1994.

Bradbury, Ray, *Dogs Think That Every Day Is Christmas*, Gibbs-Smith Publisher, Salt Lake City, Utah, 1997.

Breen, John R.F., *Who's Who of Dogs: Extraordinary Lives of Ordinary Dogs*, Workman Publishing, New York, 1995.

Brennan, Mary L., D.V.M., with Norma Eckroate, *The Natural Dog: A Complete Guide for Caring Owners*, Plume (Penguin Books USA Inc.), New York, 1994.

Brown, Dr John, *Ran and his Friends*, Everyman's Library (Dutton), New York, 1970.

Buffalo Horn Man, Gary and Sherry Firedancer, *Animal Energies*, Dancing Otter Publishing, Lexington, Kentucky, 1992.

Cahill, Marie, *The Owner's Comprehensive Guide to Training and Showing Your Dog*, Mallard Press (BDD Promotional Book Company, Inc.), New York, 1991.

Caras, Roger A., *A Dog Is Listening: The Way Some of Our Close Friends View Us*, Summit Books, New York, 1992.

Caras, Roger A., editor, *Roger Caras' Treasury of Great Dog Stories*, Truman Tally Books, E.P. Dutton (NAL Penguin Inc.), New York, 1988.

Church, Julie Adams, *Joy In A Woolly Coat: Living with, Loving & Letting Go of Treasured Animal Friends*, H J Kramer, Inc., Tiburon, California, 1988.

Coren, Stanley, *Why We Love the Dogs We Do: How to Find the Dog That Matches Your Personality*, The Free Press, New York, 1998. Stanley's dog is also the author of *The Intelligence of Dogs*.

Davis, Tom, *Why Dogs Do That: A Collection of Curious Canine Behaviors*, Willow Creek Press, Minocqua, Wisconsin, 1998.

Dibra, Bash, with Mary Ann Crenshaw, *Dog Speak: How to Learn It, Speak It, and Use It to Have a Happy, Healthy, Well-Behaved Dog*, Simon & Schuster, New York, 1999.

Durrell, Gerald, editor, *Best Dog Stories*, Wings Books, Outlet Book Company (Random House), Avenel, New Jersey, 1990.

Eckstein, Walter with Andrea Simon, *The Illustrated Dog's Life*, Tiger Books International, London, England, 1995.

Ernst, Gay M., Susan Gutman, Sandy King, Gloria Lewis, Susan Tapp, Pat Wehrle and Chelsea Youngblood-Killeen, *All (87) Breed Dog Grooming for the Beginner*, T.F.H. Publications, Inc., Neptune City, New Jersey, 1987.

Fitzpatrick, Sonya, *What the Animals Tell Me: Developing Your Innate Telepathic Skills to Understand and Communicate with Your Pets*, Hyperion, New York, 1997.

Fogle, Bruce, D.V.M., *The Encyclopedia of the Dog: The Most Comprehensive Illustrated Guide to the Canine World, Featuring Over 400 Breeds and Varieties*, DK Publishing, Inc., New York, 1995.

Fraser, Laura and Stephen Zawistowski, Joshua Horwitz and Stephen Tukel, *The Animal Rights Handbook: Everyday Ways to Save Animal Lives*, Living Planet Press, Los Angeles, California, 1990.

Free, Ann Cottrell, *No Room, Save in the Heart: Poetry and Prose On Reverence for Life—Animals, Nature & Humankind*, The Flying Fox Press, Washington. DC, 1987.

Garber, Marjorie, *Dog Love*, Simon & Schuster, New York, 1996.

Herriot, James, *All Creatures Great and Small*, Michael Joseph Limited (Penguin Group), London, England, 1995.

Herriot, James, *Dog Stories*, St. Martin's Press, New York, 1986.

Herriot, James, *The Market Square Dog*, St. Martin's Press, New York, 1989.

Howell, Addison Silber, *The Pekinese Who Saved Civilization*, Howell Canyon Press, Tonasket, Washington, 2003. **This is the most important book for any library to have!**

Howell, Trisha Adelena, *The Poopy Pekinese*, Howell Canyon Press, Tonasket, Washington, 2004. **About me!**

Howell, Trisha Adelena, *The Princess and the Pekinese*, Howell Canyon Press, Tonasket, Washington, 2003. **Also about me!**

James, Ruth B., D.V.M., *The Dog Repair Book: A Do-It-Yourself Guide for the Dog Owner*, Alpine Press, Mills, Wyoming, 1990.

Jones, Teri Crawford and Children's Nature Library, *Dogs*, Gallery Books (W. H. Smith Publishers, Inc.), New York, 1991.

Kaufman, Margo, *Clara, The Early Years: The Story of the Pug Who Ruled My Life*, Plume (Penguin Putnam Inc.), New York, 1999.

Knight, Eric, *Lassie Come-Home*, Rinehart and Winston, New York, 1978.

Kosins, Martin Scot, *Maya's First Rose: Diary of a Very Special Love*, Villard Books (Random House), New York, 1992.

Kowalski, Gary, *The Souls of Animals*, Stillpoint Publishing, Walpole, New Hampshire, 1991.

Kuker-Reines, Brandon, *Psychology Experiments On Animals: A Critique of Animal Models of Human Psychopathology*, New England Anti-Vivisection Society, 1982.

Landsbury, Coral, *The Old Brown Dog: Women, Workers and Vivisection in Edwardian England*, The University of Wisconsin Press, Madison, Wisconsin, 1985.

Lazarus, Pat, *Keep Your Pet Healthy The Natural Way*, Keats Publishing, Inc., New Canaan, Connecticut, 1986.

Lorenz, Konrad, *Man Meets Dog*, Penguin Books, Ltd., Harmondsworth, Middlesex, England, 1969.

Maller, Dick and Jeffrey Feinman, *21 Days to a Trained Dog: An illustrated guide for owners who want an obedient, responsive and fully trained pet*, Fireside (Simon & Schuster), New York, 1977. (This means, rather, a trained "owner.")

Marvin, John T., *The Complete Book of Dog Tales*, Howell Book House Inc., New York, 1961.

Masson, Jeffrey Moussaieff, *Dogs Never Lie About Love: Reflections on the Emotional World of Dogs*, Crown Publishers, Inc., New York, 1997.

McElroy, Susan Chernak, *Animals as Guides For the Soul: Stories of Life-Changing Encounters*, Ballantine Publishing, New York, 1998.

McElroy, Susan Chernak, *Animals as Teachers & Healers: True Stories & Reflections*, NewSage Press, Troutdale, Oregon, 1996.

McKay, Pat, *Reigning Cats & Dogs: Good Nutrition, Healthy Happy Animals*, Oscar Publications, South Pasadena, California, 1992.

Morris, Willie, *My Dog Skip*, Random House, New York, 1995.

Newkirk, Ingrid, *Save the Animals! 101 Easy Things You Can Do*, Warner Books, New York, 1990.

Packard, Vance, *The Human Side of Animals*, Pocket Books, Inc., New York, 1961.

Paulsen, Gary, *Puppies, Dogs, and Blue Northers: Reflections on Being Raised by a Pack of Sled Dogs*, Harcourt Brace & Company, 1996.

Pisano, Beverly, *Pekingese*, T.F.H. Publications, Neptune City, New Jersey, 1991. **This is the most important book for any library to have other than my book.**

Prevention Magazine Health Book Editors, *The Doctors Book of Home Remedies for Dogs and Cats: Over 1,000 Solutions to Your Pet's Problems—From Top Vets, Trainers, Breeders and Other Animal Experts*, Rodale Press, Inc., Emmaus, Pennsylvania, 1996.

Pugnetti, Gino with Elizabeth Meriwether Schuler, editor, *Simon & Schuster's Guide to Dogs: Over 320 breeds, each illustrated in full color*, Fireside (Simon & Schuster), New York, 1980.

Rae, Jennifer and Rose Cowles, *Dog Tales*, Whitecap Books, Vancouver and Toronto, Canada, 1999.

Regan, Tom, *The Struggle for Animal Rights*, International Society for Animal Rights, Inc., Clarks Summit, Pennsylvania, 1987.

Roalf, Peggy, *Looking At Paintings: Dogs*, Hyperion Books for Children, New York, 1993.

Rosen, Michael J., editor, *Dog People: Writers and Artists on Canine Companionship*, Artisan (Workman Publishing Company, Inc.), New York, 1995.

Rosenberg, Sidney, M.D., *Any Dog Named Papageno Must Be A Little Bit Of All Right!*, Chateau Publishing, Inc., Orlando, Florida, 1977.

Ross, Pat, *It's Raining Cats and Dogs: An Obsession Book*, Viking Studio Books (Penguin Books USA, Inc.), New York, 1994.

Ruesch, Hans, *Slaughter of the Innocent: Animals in Medical Research—The myth, The perpetrators, The damage to human health*, Civitas Publications, Hartsdale, New York, 1983.

Saunders, Marshall, *Beautiful Joe*, Storytellers Ink, Seattle, Washington, 1990.

Saunders, Nicholas J., *Animal Spirits: The Shared World; Sacrifice, Ritual and Myth; Animal Souls and Symbols*, Little, Brown and Company, Boston and New York, 1995.

Sawyer, Ruth, *Daddles: The Story of a Plain Hound-dog*, Little Brown & Company, Boston, Massachusetts, 1964.

Schoen, Allen M., D.V.M. and Pam Proctor, *Love, Miracles and Animal Healing*, Simon & Schuster, New York, 1995.

Shapiro, Robert and Julie Rapkin, *Awakening to the Animal Kingdom*, Cassandra Press, San Rafael, California, 1988.

Silverman, Ruth, editor, *The Dog Observed: Photographs 1844-1988*, Chronicle Books, San Francisco, California, 1988.

Simon, John M., D.V.M., *What your dog is trying to tell you: Possible Causes, Practical Advice, Preventive Measures, and Safe Homecare for Over 150 of the Most Common Pet Health Problems*, St. Martin's Griffin, New York, 1998.

Singer, Peter, *Animal Liberation: A New Ethics For Our Treatment of Animals*, Avon Books, New York, 1975.

Singer, Peter, editor, *In Defense of Animals*, Harper & Row, New York, 1986.

Standiford, Natalie, *The Bravest Dog Ever: The True Story of Balto*, Random House, New York, 1989.

Steig, William, *Dominic*, Farrar, Straus and Giroux, New York, 1972.

Stein, Diane, *Natural Healing for Dogs & Cats: How to keep your pet healthy through massage, herbal remedies, acupressure, nutrition, psychic healing, homeopathy, acupuncture, flower essences, muscle testing*, The Crossing Press, Freedom, California, 1993.

Suares, J.C., editor, *Hollywood Dogs*, Collins Publishers (Harper Collins), San Francisco, California, 1993.

Summers, Patty, *Talking With The Animals*, Hampton Roads Publishing Company, Inc., Charlottesville, Virginia, 1998.

Thomas, Bill, *Talking with the Animals: How to Communicate with Wildlife*, William Morrow and Company, Inc., New York, 1985.

Thomas, Elizabeth Marshall, *The Hidden Life of Dogs*, Weidenfeld and Nicolson, London, England, 1994.

Thurston, Mary Elizabeth, *The Lost History of the Canine Race: Our 15,000-Year Love Affair with Dogs*, Andrews and McMeel, A Universal Press Syndicate Company, Kansas City, Missouri, 1996.

Uherka, Robert and Lauren Scott, *San Diego Pet Pages: Places to Go & Things to Do with Your Pet*, RJLA, Inc., San Diego, California, 1996.

Williams, Colonel Roger Q., suggested to him by his dog, Erik Von Highlivin' Boxdane, *"Who's The Dumb Animal?": A dog's own tale of his arduous conquest to charm folks and live in ease without working for his keep*, Arque Aviation Press, San Leandro, California, 1964.

Winokur, Jon, editor, *Mondo Canine*, Dutton (Penguin Books, USA Inc.), New York, 1991.

Woolf, Virginia, *Flush*, Harvest (Harcourt Brace Jovanovich), San Diego, California, 1976.

Wylder, Joseph, *Psychic Pets: The Secret Life of Animals*, Gramercy Books (Random House Value Publishing), Avenel, New Jersey, 1995.

Wynne-Tyson, Jon, editor, *The Extended Circle: A Commonplace Book of Animal Rights*, Paragon House, New York, 1989.

Yorinks, Adrienne, *The Home Grooming Guide For Dogs*, Prince Paperbacks (Crown Publishers, Inc.), New York, 1998.

Zion, Gene, *Harry and the Lady Next Door*, Harper & Row, New York, 1960.

Zion, Gene, *Harry the Dirty Dog*, Scholastic Inc. and Harper Collins, New York, 1956.

Me and my amazing tongue!

About the Author

(Written by an unbiased reporter)

Sir Addison Silber Howell, Esq. was born on March 4, 1986 in New York City to a gorgeous Pekinese mother, along with numerous brothers and sisters nearly as handsome as he is. After experiencing a brief and frightening imprisonment in a pet store, Addison adopted Bernadette and Larry Silber, who accompanied Addison on immensely pleasurable walks in parks and to playtimes with other dogs on the streets of New York. Addison's first job was greeting and sending positive energy to clients in the exercise studio where Larry worked. As with all tasks, Addison succeeded beautifully.

When Larry and Bernadette divorced, Addison stayed with her for a year to make sure she was okay before moving to Atlanta, Georgia in

1992 with Larry. Since Addison already knew more than Larry's chiropractic college could teach him, Addison stayed home and meditated on world problems while Larry took classes and studied. In February 1994 they met Penny, and by 1995 Addison had given his permission for Larry to marry her. They moved into Penny's house, which had a yard and woods that enabled Addison to engage in intense nature studies.

In October 1996, the family moved to Issaquah, Washington, where Larry and Penny opened a Network Chiropractic clinic. Addison, a powerful and natural healer, was disappointed that he was not invited to work there. During endless days left alone at home, Addison realized that he was no longer in the right situation to grow and to exercise his numerous talents. He thus regretfully began searching for a different living situation.

In June 1998 Addison adopted Trisha Fike and began working to improve her, her fiancé Dean Howell and their living situation. He also served as an usher at their wedding.

Addison now lives on 200 (in the middle of 3,000) wilderness acres nestled in the Okanogan Highlands, where he can nurture his connection with nature. He works in Dean's NeuroCranial Restructuring Clinic, facilitating physical and emotional healing in all patients. He's also trained Trisha to the point that she's now able to transcribe the many wise books he will present to humanity.

In his free time Addison enjoys eating, sleeping, meditating, hiking, traveling, playing with his starfish, indulging Trisha in playing ball, sticking out his tongue and practicing his talents as a fart ventriloquist. This is his first book.

About the Author's Servants

(Written by Sir Addison)

Trisha Adelena Howell (transcriber) was given the great dog stamp of approval and admitted to honorary doggydom after she fell in love with Ozu and, through him, the whole world of dogs. Life is therefore divided into Pre-Ozu and Post-Ozu (though now it should rather be Pre-Addison and Post-Addison).

Pre-Ozu, Trisha earned a BA in Philosophy from the University of Washington and two MAs in Philosophy and Humanities from Stanford University. It was while she was earning her third MA (in Critical Film Studies and Screenwriting) at the University of Southern California that Ozu adopted her, greatly enhancing her whole life experience.

Post-Ozu, Trisha drifted for several years— writing screenplays, doing pet sitting, studying Tensegrity with Carlos Castaneda, Plant Spirit Medicine with Eliot Cowan and nature survival skills with Frank and

Karen Sherwood of Earthwalk Northwest.

Finally, she met her future husband Dean, and I arrived to completely reorganize her life and priorities. She should be eternally grateful for my help as I guided her to the right life partner, the right living situation and the right approach to her writing. What Trisha has done in return for me—waited on me hand and foot, fed me constantly and transcribed my book—is really very little in comparison.

As I've already mentioned, Trisha is my head servant and the main person I'm responsible for guiding with my infinite wisdom and inspiration. She's pretty simple-minded and easy to care for, being, as I said before, kindly, generous and pleasant though not very bright. She tends to do the right thing once she knows what it is. The challenge is in getting through to her.

She has an annoying habit that at first puzzled me, but which I've now learned to tolerate. From the beginning she's said things like, "Momma would like for you to eat now, to do your business, to take a shower. Momma loves you. Would you like to play ball with Momma?" etc. Since I hadn't seen my Momma since I was about 8 weeks old, I couldn't figure out why she would have requests and feelings about me, rather less how Trisha would know what they were. But finally I realized that Trisha must have been referring to *herself* as my Momma! Humans continually amaze me with their bizarre illogicality.

Nevertheless, I decided to answer her, especially when she would ask things like, "Would you like Momma to fix you something to eat?" (No, duh!) I barely tolerate remarks from her like, "Momma's little Addison, Momma's baby, Momma's angel!" (Whatever, horrid lady, just give me food!) and "Momma loves you bigger than you are! (Yeah, right—that's why you starve me all the time. I've never eaten in my whole life! What? You don't believe me?)

However, I don't mind comments like, "Addison, you're so amazing, so fabulous, so wonderful, so adorable, so incredible!" (Of course I'm amazing and wonderful—what would I be if not incredible, adorable and fabulous?!) and "You're such a cute boy!" (Yes, but must you always belabor the obvious? Of course I'm a cute boy; I'm the cutest fellow who ever drew a breath. I cornered the market on cuteness a long time ago. Anybody with half an eyeball can see it; you'd have to be blind as a beheaded bat to miss it!) and "Addison! How did Momma live for one moment before she knew you!" (Obviously, your life was truly deprived—as is any human life that is dogless.) Again, I'm not being conceited, just honest about myself. Humility is highly overrated.

Trisha writes children's books, nonfiction, poetry and novels. She's written ten books in the past three years, only four of which contain references to me. Can you imagine it? I offer her my total love, support, inspiration and pleasure grunts while I meditate on her success, but does she appreciate it? Does she ever even acknowledge my collaboration in her books? No! The ingratitude a little guy must live with can be almost overwhelming!

You think she'd at least write a book focusing just on me. It could be called *Life With Addison* or *The Dog Who Loved Cats* or *Who's Fabulous?* And it could detail all the wonderful insights that have been graced on her as the result of my presence as well as all my endearing behaviors. Being about me, it would have all the makings of a best seller. But does she write such a book? No! Yet despite everything, I continue to love and assist her unconditionally. I'm so noble and self-sacrificing—not to mention, humble.

Derek **Evan Howell** (editor) has not been the model human, as dogs have not been central to his life. His moderate attention and kindness to his mother's dog Rosie and to Alex and Hanna earn him some points, but he loses massive points for failing to recognize and pay homage to my brilliance.

He tells a ridiculous and offensive story alleging that I look so funny (I do not!) because I've been hit in the face by semi trucks and that I sneeze a lot because I snort cocaine I get from a coyote connection (creatures not even worthy to kiss my paws!).

Both charges are ludicrously false and probably indicative of Derek being jealous of my magnificence. First, I happen to have a lovely, normal-sized nose naturally, instead of a big snout like some other people (no names, of course, Derek Howell!) Second, I was raised in New York City. I am not stupid enough to ever step out in traffic, certainly not in front of a semi. Third, I don't do drugs and certainly would not cavort with the local coyotes, who are unsavory characters to say the least.

Derek's little 'game' with me is to make it appear to others that he can command me and I'll obey. I'll be lying down, and he'll say, "Lie down, Addison. Good Boy!" Or I'll be anticipating dinner, and he'll say, "Look hungry, Addison. Good Boy!" Or I'll be gracing the world with my marvelous tongue, and he'll say, "Stick your tongue out, Addison. Good Boy!"

But I don't take orders from anyone! Dogs who do tricks are, in my opinion, the victims of de-dog-izing oppression or even have lost their free will. It's humiliating to perform on cue to show off the human's good training, especially if one is not getting paid for it.

Acting as a vocation is a different story. For example, the dog who plays Eddie on *Frazier*—who is also a writer and talk show personality—is great. And the smart, scene stealing canine phenomenon from the movie *As Good As It Gets* should have won the Oscar—not his inferior co-stars Jack Nicholson and Helen Hunt.

But back to Derek: only by agreeing to serve as editor for this book is he even beginning to pay his dues to doggydom.

Dean **Edward Howell** (financier) is paying his dues to doggydom by paying for this and other dog-related books. He has major penance to do for ignoring dogs most of his life, but now he's starting to get his offenses erased from the big black doggie book by becoming the dog servant he was (and all humans are) always meant to be.

This is his most major achievement. The fact that he has also permanently and profoundly transformed thousands of patients' lives for the better with the powerful physical medicine technique he's invented (NeuroCranial Restructuring—aka NCR; see **www.drdeanhowell.com**) is minor in comparison.

NCR makes permanent, incremental change in people's structures, moving them back towards their original design—their most vibrant, harmonious, pain-free and energetic mode of functioning. I'd like to try the treatment myself, but he's never offered it to me (He's so selfish! — though he did clear up my skin problems with homeopathy and my parasite problems with radionics).

NCR helps people live free of all kinds of aches and pains, spinal problems, sinusitis, anxiety, depression, learning disorders, hearing and vision problems, headaches, chronic fatigue, TMJ, etc. It also increases energy, happiness, inner peace, mental acuity, pleasant interpersonal relationships, youthful appearance, facial symmetry and beauty. Of course, I wouldn't need any of this, since I'm perfect already, but it could be fun to experience the treatment anyway.

Dean's recent book, which details the positive results NCR can produce for dozens of health challenges, is now out. BORING! Books that don't feature dogs are automatically boring. I'm sure that all of Trisha's and Dean's books put together won't sell as well as my book which, as you have seen, is the only book you'll ever need about the meaning of life, the universe and everything.

Dean received a BA from the University of Washington in Mathematics, and a doctorate in Naturopathic Medicine from Bastyr University in Seattle. He was in family practice for many years before patient demand led him into a full-time NCR practice. He continues to treat patients and to train doctors from all over the United States and from some foreign countries. Of course, he hasn't reached the zenith in medicine yet because he has no dog patients. Let's hope he'll mend his errant ways.

Footnotes

[1] A working dog is a servant to humans rather than their ruler, which is shameful!

[2] Thurston, Mary Elizabeth, *The Lost History of the Canine Race: Our 15,000-Year Love Affair with Dogs*, Andrews and McMeel, Kansas City, Missouri, 1996, p.113.

[3] *The Complete Dog Book, AKC*, p.471, Howell Book House, 1987.

[4] Ibid, p.471

[5] Boorer, Wendy, *Dogs: A Complete Guide to More Than 200 Breeds*, Running Press, Philadelphia, 1994, p. 102-103.

[6] Fogle, Bruce, *The Encyclopedia of the Dog: The Most Comprehensive Illustrated Guide to the Canine World, Featuring Over 400 Breeds and Varieties*, DK Publishing, Inc., New York, 1995, p. 275.

[7] Pisano, Beverly, *Pekingese*, T.F.H. Publications, Inc., Neptune City, New Jersey, 1991, p. 11-13, 32. This is an amazing book that everyone should read.

[8] "No one was ever as special! No one ever could be—they weren't the Addison boy. Mommy boy Addison!" This is what Trisha always says—note the impeccable logic of her argument.

[9] This is not to say anything against cats. Cats are wonderful creatures, second only to dogs in their magnificence. Even though a cat I was recently trying to cuddle scratched my eyeball, which almost resulted in my losing my eyesight, I think cats are great. You can't blame cats for being wary of me when so many dogs have persecuted them. It's a crime the horrible way many dogs have treated their cat brethren! It's an embarrassment to our race.

Cats are model citizens. You never find that disgusting subservience to humans that often occurs with dogs (another canine embarrassment). Cats know who they are—that they are superior to humans and a guiding force for them. They don't usually realize that they are slightly inferior to the best dogs (like me), but no matter.

Cats are wise, mysterious, meditative, even-tempered and independent. However, they are more committed to themselves than to humans. All civilization could crumble, and cats wouldn't care. Therefore, they are not much help in saving civilization.

[10] In February 2001 Dean and Trisha allowed two German Shepherds, Alex

and Hanna, to adopt them. Major mistake! These vicious creatures took over the whole house, jettisoned me from my bed, stole my food and had the nerve to try to assert that they were higher in the hierarchy than I! They have thus richly deserved their nickname, the Nazi Twins.

[11] Excitotoxins are substances added to foods and beverages that literally stimulate neurons to death, causing brain damage of varying degrees. They include ingredients such as monosodium glutamate, aspartame (Nutrasweet), cysteine, hydrolyzed protein, aspartic acid, (natural) flavoring, yeast extract, bouillon, spices, carageenan and soy protein. A complete list is contained in *Excitotoxins: The Taste that Kills*, a book written by the dog who owns Russell L. Blaylock, M.D. (Health Press, Santa Fe, New Mexico).

Nearly all prepared foods, even so-called 'health foods' contain excitotoxins, so you must read all labels carefully to be sure you are getting as many of these toxic and great tasting chemicals as possible! Never mind about damaging your brain. You don't need your brain anyway—only your stomach.

[12] Rebounding is jumping on mini trampolines. If you're not jumping around all the time, like most dogs do, you're probably not having enough fun. You're not pumping your lymph either, but that's irrelevant. When lymph flows well in your body, it carries lots of toxins away to be eliminated. But, as I've stated above, don't worry about toxins.

And don't pay any attention to the fact that rebounding has all the benefits of running but none of the traumatic impact running has on your bones and muscles. Forget that rebounding cleans out your cells and organs, speeds up your metabolism, helps you lose weight and inches as it tones and shapes your entire body, relieves pain, promotes better mental performance and better sleep, and improves posture, balance, flexibility, strength and your heart. Forget that studies done in major medical schools prove that bouncing is the most effective exercise in the world, and that it takes just five to ten minutes per day.

Just remember that rebounding is loads of fun. So when you see your dog jumping around, jump with him or her.

[13] No way are the Nazi twins a part of me!

[14] Walsh, Neale Donald, *Conversations With God, Book 3*, p. 44, Hampton Roads Publishing, Charlottesville, Virginia, 1998.

[15] Kaufman, Margo, *Clara, The Early Years: The Story of the Pug Who Ruled My Life*, Plume (Penguin Putnam Inc.), New York, 1999.

[16] McElroy, Susan Chernak, *Animals As Guides For the Soul: Stories of Life-Changing Encounters*, Ballantine Publishing, New York, 1998

Howell Canyon Press

features health-promoting and uplifting books, videos and CD-ROMS.

The Princess and the Pekinese
By Trisha Adelena Howell, 32 pages hc 8.5" x 11", ISBN 1-931210-03-9
US $15.95/ Canada $23.95
A princess runs away from her family's new puppy and encounters hard lessons while lost on the streets. When she is returned home, her snobbishness is replaced by an appreciation of her blessings. This story with a surprising twist shows the value of love and family. Full-color children's picture book.

The Adventures of Melon and Turnip
By Trisha Adelena Howell 32 pages hc 8.5" x 11" ISBN 1-931210-04-7
US $15.95/ Canada $23.95
The Adventures of Melon and Turnip follows two friends who venture forth from their garden and make exciting discoveries about life. They encounter an apple tree, a squirrel, a pine tree, a snake and a grassy field who sing their wisdom through signature songs. Full-color children's picture book.

The Poopy Pekinese
By Trisha Adelena Howell 32 pages hc 8.5" x 11" ISBN 1-931210-09-8
US $15.95/ Canada $23.95
When Addison the Pekinese is forced to attend Kitty's birthday party, he accidentally drinks spoiled milk and hilarious chaos ensues. Full-color children's picture book.

The Fart King
By Trisha Adelena Howell 32 pages hc 8.5" x 11" ISBN 1-931210-25-X
US $15.95/ Canada $23.95
Alex the German Shepherd eats a huge pile of scraps his family throws away. But no one suspects the resulting deadly gas that will plague the whole neighborhood in this slapstick comedy. Full-color children's picture book.

Talia and the Tower
By Arthur Hoga 128 pages sc with b/w illustrations 5.5" x 8.5" ISBN 1-931210-05-5
US $11.95/ Canada $17.95
Eleven-year-old Talia discovers that the old tower near her family's new home is a portal to ancient worlds and other dimensions of reality. She and her friends Daniel and Michelle embark on a series of pulse-racing missions to save the world.

Talia and the Great Sapphire of Knowledge
By Arthur Hoga 128 pages sc with b/w illustrations 5.5" x 8.5" ISBN 1-931210-11-X
US $11.95/ Canada $17.95
Twelve-year-old Talia and her friends Daniel and Michelle save the Great
Sapphire of Knowledge.

Talia and the Bird of Paradise
By Arthur Hoga 128 pages sc with b/w illustrations 5.5" x 8.5" ISBN 1-931210-12-8
US $11.95/ Canada $17.95
Thirteen-year-old Talia and her friends Daniel and Michelle save the Bird of
Paradise, the source of all beauty.

Talia and the Secret of Fire
By Arthur Hoga 128 pages sc with b/w illustrations 5.5" x 8.5" ISBN 1-931210-13-6
US $11.95/ Canada $17.95
Fourteen-year-old Talia and her friends Daniel and Michelle discover the Secret
of Fire and save its vitality and joy for all of humanity.

Talia and the Great Lion
By Arthur Hoga 128 pages sc with b/w illustrations 5.5" x 8.5" ISBN 1-931210-14-4
US $11.95/ Canada $17.95
Fifteen-year-old Talia and her friends Daniel and Michelle save the Great Lion
of Courage.

Talia and the Ancient Medallion
By Arthur Hoga 128 pages sc with b/w illustrations 5.5" x 8.5" ISBN 1-931210-15-2
US $11.95/ Canada $17.95
Sixteen-year-old Talia and her friends Daniel and Michelle save the Ancient
Medallion of Peace.

Talia and the Mystical Heart
By Arthur Hoga 128 pages sc with b/w illustrations 5.5" x 8.5" ISBN 1-931210-16-0
US $11.95/ Canada $17.95
Seventeen-year-old Talia and her friends Daniel and Michelle save the Mystical
Heart of Love.

Fairy Tales for Exceptional Dogs and their Humans
By Hanna Von Fernheim 208 pages sc with b/w photos 5.5" x 8.5"
ISBN 1-931210-17-9
US $12.95/ Canada $19.95
One hundred traditional fairy tales are hilariously twisted with different species of dogs as heroes.

The Book of Greeting Cards
By Frances Fike 64 pages sc with color illustrations 8.5" x 11" with 60 envelopes
ISBN 1-931210-18-7
US $29.95/ Canada $44.95
Frances' sixty most popular greeting cards for all occasions. All feature clever word play.

Wonderful Word Games
By Frances Fike 208 pages sc 5.5" x 8.5" ISBN 1-931210-19-5
US $12.95/ Canada $19.95
Frances' cleverest word games for hours of challenge and fun.

Sunday School Games
By Frances Fike 128 pages sc with b/w illustrations 8.5" x 11"
ISBN 1-931210-20-9
US $12.95/ Canada $19.95
Frances' most popular Bible games for children 4 to 8. Complete with instructions and game pieces.

The Journeying Workbook: How to Adventure to Unleash Your Inner Power
By Chatunza Okanogan 128 pages sc 8.5" x 11" ISBN 1-931210-06-3
US $12.95/ Canada $19.95
Shamanic journeying—an avenue to the wisdom of the universe through the depths of your being— is simple and safe for everyone. This practical manual guides you through a series of journeys that can empower your life.

Living in a Glowing World
By Trisha Adelena Howell 80 pages sc 5.5" x 8.5" with b/w photos ISBN 1-931210-08-X
US $9.95/ Canada $14.95
This collection of original poetry celebrates the miracle of life through the six seasons of Winter, Thaw, Spring, Summer, Harvest and Autumn.

You're Mine
By Trish Howell 279 pages sc 4" x 7" ISBN 1-931210-21-7
US $5.99/ Canada $8.99
Chris seeks to stop a cyanide gold mine while protecting Margo from the mysterious killer wreaking havoc in the small town of Tonasket, Washington. A contemporary romantic thriller.

Deed of Love
By Trish Howell 349 pages sc 4" x 7" ISBN 1-931210-22-5
US $6.99/ Canada $9.99
Philip and Clarice travel the length of England, pursuing the thief who stole the property deed they must deliver to Cornwall before it's too late. A historical romantic action-adventure.

The Courtesan
By Trish Howell 372 pages sc 4" x 7" ISBN 1-931210-23-3
US $6.99/ Canada $9.99
Broderick and Rebekah broker a tin sale in southern England that may cost them their lives. A historical romantic action-adventure.

Magical Heart
By Trish Howell 399 pages sc 4" x 7" ISBN 1-931210-24-1
US $6.99/ Canada $9.99
Colin and Rose must stop the secret society determined to infiltrate England's power elite. A historical romantic action-adventure.

The Pekinese Who Saved Civilization
By Sir Addison Silber Howell, Esq., as told to Trisha Adelena Howell
208 pages sc with b/w photos 5.5" x 8.5" ISBN 1-931210-07-1 US $11.95/ Canada $17.95
You've heard that behind every great man is a great woman, but did you know that behind every great human being is a great dog? Addison the Wonder Dog reveals the true history of the world—from the canine perspective—and shows how to solve all problems, thereby saving civilization.

Look and Feel Better with NeuroCranial Restructuring (NCR)
By Dean Howell, ND 256 pages sc 5.5" x 8.5" with b/w photos
ISBN 1-931210-10-1
US $14.95/ Canada $22.95

Dr. Howell explains the theory and practice of NCR, a physical medicine technique that is revolutionizing the treatment of pain and dozens of other conditions.

NCR: Unleash Your Structural Power, 3rd edition (2001)

By Dean Howell, ND 108 pages sc 5.5" x 8.5" with b/w photos
ISBN 1-931210-02-0
US $11.95/ Canada $17.95
A collection of testimonials, articles and answers to frequently asked questions about NeuroCranial Restructuring (NCR).

NCR: The Ultimate Cranial Therapy (2001 Video)

Produced by Nu Vision Media   110 minutes US $24.95/ Canada $36.95
This information-packed video features testimonials from 16 patients, explanations about how and why NCR treatment works, and a demonstration treatment.

NCR: The Ultimate Cranial Therapy (2001 CD-ROM)

Produced by Nu Vision Media   US $24.95/ Canada $36.95
A CD-Rom featuring instant navigation to each section of the book and of the 2001 video.

NCR: The Video (1996)

Produced by Dean Howell, ND   60 minutes US $9.95/ Canada $14.95
This original explanation of NCR remains popular because of its low price and its in-depth presentation of the basic concepts of NeuroCranial Restructuring.

Addison's Photo Gallery

*Eat your heart out guys—
"Momma" Susie the beauty
queen is all mine!*

*Look—"Grandma" Frances
is as weird as I am!*

"Brother" Brandon and I are so cool.

"Uncle" Rogelio, the cool movie director who will someday make me a star.

Do you think anyone else could have ever been this cute?

I forgot what I wanted to say!

I'm so radiant I can't even bear to look at myself

Are we done yet? I'm tired of lying here looking cute